· a midnight carol ·

Patricia K. Davis

◆

St. Martin's Press ❧ *New York*

a
midnight
carol

♦

A NOVEL OF HOW

CHARLES DICKENS

SAVED CHRISTMAS

Frontispiece: Charles Dickens. *The Illustrated London
News*, April 8, 1843. *Courtesy The Library of Congress*

Library of Congress Cataloging-in-Publication Data

Davis, Patricia K.
    A midnight carol : a novel of how Charles Dickens
    saved Christmas /
Patricia K. Davis. — 1st ed.
        p.   cm.
    ISBN 0-312-24523-8
    1. Dickens, Charles, 1812–1870—Fiction.   I. Title.
PS3554.A937615M54   1999
813' .54—dc21   99-15886
                                                                          CIP

First Edition: November 1999

10   9   8   7   6   5   4   3   2   1

Book design by Claire Naylon Vaccaro

CHAPTER ONE

here comes a time in many a man's life when, no matter how hard he has worked, how honestly he has labored, how bravely he has tried to defend his beliefs, he ought to consider giving up.

The winter of 1843 was just such a time in the life of one Londoner. With the odds mounting against him, common sense dictated that he turn to and lead a conventional life. His other choice was to stay the course, pushing himself to the very limits of his character and courage, and risk losing everything in pursuit of his goal. Do or die.

And therein lies the tale.

Day by day, darkness came earlier, enveloping the land and the souls who lived upon it. In these northern climes, the long and languid days of summer yielded each fall to fast-approaching night. By December, the sun forsook the sky by late afternoon, taking with it heat and hope. Then cold blew in with its polar breath, hardening the ground—and human hearts—from the icy Orkneys to barren Dartmoor.

Centuries had passed since the reign of Henry II's "merry old" England. Little about Britain was now very merry; *dreary* was the world. The year 1843 loomed as desolate and colorless a time as the United Kingdom had ever seen. Children felt old and the old felt dead; others were too tired to feel anything at all.

The people of Britain were unsettled, trapped in the shift from the familiar comforts of shire and farm to the hardships of sullen, infested cities. Along the way they had lost their signposts to the past, their sense of connection to tradition and lore. They owned nothing in the present and dared not hope—not these slum dwellers of newly industrialized England—for a future.

Life offered little relief from the bleakness. The privileged few might enjoy festivities, but workers and their families knew nothing of holidays. Long, long before, England had celebrated Christmas with its twelve days and nights of unbridled joy. No more. Christmas was a workday like any other, its merrymaking all but forgotten.

Still, in this fathomless dark, light found its way. Like the life force in a grass shoot boring through brickwork, the spirit of giving would find its path. It would settle into the soul of our beleaguered Londoner and breathe into his being the spirit of Christmas. It would not come easily, this miracle of belief, but summon and tax all his powers.

He lived in what appeared to be a thriving household, One Devonshire Terrace, across from Regent's Park. To some, the house looked haunted, a hulking mass of mismatched stone; to others, it appeared cheery with its front door and railings painted a bright green, the master's favorite color. Green, too, was the square-walled garden, a small oasis in the grimy gray city.

Looking at the house, a visitor would not have guessed that its leaseholder payments were three months overdue.

The guardian of the green door was the family's one-of-a-kind butler, Albert Boodle. Eighty, dyspeptic, bedeviled by bunions, he refused to acknowledge his severe nearsightedness. He was at that moment struggling to set the hands of a grandfather clock for a time zone known only to him.

Like Mrs. Minnie Plimpton, the family's housekeeper and nanny, Boodle hadn't seen wages in roughly six weeks.

Mrs. Plimpton, presently engaged in the kitchen, was bargaining with the milkman for another week's provision, although she had nothing left with which she might barter.

In their upstairs bedrooms and playroom, the household's four children gamboled in clothing that didn't fit, so fast were they outgrowing their garments. None was yet six years old. The youngest was an infant, one was still a toddler.

In the downstairs study, the lady of the household pored over ledgers, struggling to decide what she might pare. Had their budget been a seesaw, the family income would have been suspended high in air, with the family bills bottoming out on the ground.

And she had news for her husband due home shortly from delivering a speech at the Atheneum. She had not been ill that morning, no. The physician had come and told her straightaway that she suffered not from the grippe or any kind of ague but from a condition she had experienced before. Four times before, to be exact.

The young master's health was also rocky. More frequently came the spasms, colic, seizures, headaches, depression, and biting neuralgia that left him abed and envying the dead their peaceable, painless sleep.

He never complained, not about his father, who exploited him at every turn, and not about his mother, who assumed that her son should give his all and expect nothing in return.

Neither did the master of One Devonshire suspect

that his publishing ventures were speeding toward collapse. He hadn't a guinea in earnings to expect and didn't even know it. Far from it. He actually thought that his next project would prove a triumph. After all, his previous undertakings had succeeded famously. Being only thirty-one years of age, he could not imagine that his chosen career teetered on the brink of failure.

Throughout the winter of this woeful year, he experienced one reversal after another until that night he stood upon Blackfriars Bridge, stared into the offal-choked Thames, and very nearly hurled into the mucky waterway his top hat and gloves, his high hopes and plans, his will to live, and any real chance that the merry old Christmas of more enchanted times might come once again to his beloved London.

But he did come home, this unsuspecting and hopeful young father named Charles John Huffam Dickens.

Through the front door of One Devonshire Terrace, Charles bounded, exuding the storm front of energy that gave his personality such a turbulent air. He called out a greeting to his butler, who only sighed in reply. Boodle did manage to retrieve his master's cane, gloves, and hat, though Dickens kept with him a small bouquet of flowers he had bought.

Into the hallway swept the plucky housekeeper, holding in her arms the infant Walter and leading the toddler Katey by the hand. "Oh, Mr. Dickens!" Mrs. Plimpton beamed. Did they like your speech? I bet they did! I bet they was impressed!"

Katey rushed, squealing, right into her father's arms. Dickens swept her up into the air. "Kateydid, Kateydid. How high can you fly?" Katey crowed happily, but the housekeeper scolded. Behind them, Boodle aimed for the cane rack but missed. Dickens's fine walking stick hit the floor and rolled away. Boodle followed it as fast as his rheumatoid limbs would allow.

Terribly pleased with himself, Dickens told his housekeeper, "Well, well, well. It went very well indeed. My audience was quite receptive to my message, even if I did preach to the converted. Book readers are bound to accept more readily what I have to say about education."

Dickens had done more than earn acceptance from his audience. He had in fact enraptured a roomful of swooning ladies who had hung on to his every phrase, enthralled by his theatrical delivery. With his luxuriant waves of dark brown hair and glittering, searchlight eyes, Dickens commanded attention like a lead actor onstage.

As Katey chortled her happiness, two more Dickens children rushed the hallway, running down the staircase and shouting all the way. Charley and Mamie, five and four, adored their father, who spoiled them. "Papa, Papa! You're home. Was the queen there? Did you bring us treats?" The two oldest children jockeyed for position, shoving Katey facedown on all fours.

Dickens quickly mastered the mob scene. "Whoa, wait! One little Dickens at a time! Charley, hands out of your pockets and don't torture your sisters. Mamie, the queen was otherwise engaged. She had an appointment with the King of Hearts." Dickens reveled in these encounters with his children, so fresh from God, he believed. For a man of his times, Dickens held an uncommon attitude, other fathers keeping a cool distance from their offspring.

Mamie giggled while Charley made a rude noise. Behind her father's back, Katey leisurely pulled petals from the cut flowers Dickens held. Boodle wafted back into the hallway, asked absentmindedly, "Shall I tell Mrs. Dickens that you are home, sir?"

In the midst of his happy melee, Dickens laughed, "I think she knows that by now! Mrs. Plimpton, is Mrs. Dickens any better?"

The housekeeper wisely muzzled herself. "It would seem so, sir. She says she has something to tell you."

Dickens nodded, then looked at his flowers, a bedraggled, beheaded bunch of stems. He looked at his younger daughter, then back at the flowers.

"She loves me, she loves me not!" he teased.

In Charley's study, Catherine Dickens sat at an oversized oaken desk. Though cluttered, the room appeared obsessively neat, the lair of an organized though hungry mind.

Floor-to-ceiling bookshelves stocked with handsomely bound volumes lined the walls. A window over the desk looked out onto the garden, seasonally bereft of their flowers. Entering with an ebullient "Hullo, Catherine!" Charles found his wife studying their ledgers.

She looked at him with the faint smile of the insecure. In her lilting Scottish burr, Catherine called, "Hullo, Charles."

Dickens walked to his wife and kissed her on the forehead, then brought forth his mutilated bouquet. She laughed as she asked, "He loves me not?" His expression, playful at first, gave his reply, but turned grave upon seeing the accounting books.

Catherine tracked their finances and did a keen job of it. The levelheaded daughter of a hysterical mother, she considered it her job to oversee a family and maintain equilibrium. Always calm in a crisis, her placid nature counterbalanced Charley's, so excitable and haunted by fears. Sometimes her unshakable composure annoyed Charles, forcing him to bury feelings that later found life on the page.

Without prompting, Charles offered, "My royalties are overdue from the publisher. I'll be seeing them on Friday. That's income upon which we can always depend." He knew they were mired in financial quicksand with no one in sight to throw them a rope.

She encouraged him with a brave smile and a soft look from her beautiful blue eyes. It worked. He continued, "Did I tell you about the new book? I know I'll get a large advance on it!" He began roaming about the room, straightening up, turning objects first one way and then another, reorienting a lamp or inspecting silver pieces for tarnish.

Catherine watched him for a moment, then said, "The doctor came this afternoon."

Dickens stopped. His wife's health, yes. "What did he tell you?" he asked.

Catherine looked out onto the garden as she said, "He told me I am with child."

She did not see her stunned husband step involuntarily backward and grab a standing lamp for support. Instead, she saw their nuisance raven flutter onto a branch and, head cocked, stare back at her. A familiar pest, the bird flapped his wings, then settled in for the night.

After dinner, Dickens retreated to his study. He had found the meal an embarrassment. Catherine and Mrs. Plimpton had so obviously stretched the mutton, serving it with stale bread and moldy potatoes. Dickens had escaped, encamped at his desk, littered now with scrips of blue paper. Doodles, deletions, and numbers disfigured the pages. Sometimes words came to him with enormous difficulty and he wrote slowly and with painstaking care. Other times the words flowed so torrentially that his hand could barely keep pace with his head. Tonight the words did not come.

In blue ink he wrote the name "Chuzzlewig," but lined it through. In succession he dashed off Chubblewig, Chuzzletoe, Chuzzlebog, but deleted them all. Exasperated, he wadded the paper and tossed it away. Next he scribbled Sweezleden, Sweezlebach, Sweezlewag. As he struggled with the scansion of names, he heard the doorbell ring. A muffled but unmistakable voice arrested Dickens altogether. He froze. Footfalls. Boodle knocking, calling through the door, "Sir, it's—"

Ire flashed across Charley's features. Voice raised, he replied, "I know who it is, Boodle!"

In the drawing room, John Dickens sauntered about, appraising with a canny eye the room's plush and polished appointments—luxurious curtains, chairs of rosewood, sofa covered in exquisite silk. Expensive mirrors hung on the walls along with a handful of fine watercolors and oils. The piano, by contrast, seemed a cheap piece, and this drew a sneer from John.

Upon hearing his son enter, John spun around and flashed a Fagin's smile. "Charles!" he exclaimed, and strode across the room, heartily slapping his son on the back. Dickens winced, then gave his father as critical a once-over as his father had given the room. Before him stood a tall man of fading looks for his fifty-seven years, with thinning hair and thickening middle. His weight gain had aged him further so that the stubborn chin now looked like a mastiff's. Once a dashing figure, John Dickens appeared as a ghost of his former self. Charles prayed that he would escape a similar fate.

"What are you doing here, father? We had an arrangement." Charley's steely tone sliced through his father's affected manners.

John pursed his lips. "Oh yes, very kind of you to pay me to leave London. And sheer charity on your part to find me and the missus a cottage *and furnish it with salvage.*" Sarcasm flowed like venom from a cobra—smoothly, sharply, true to his nature. "I just thought I owed myself a visit to One Devonshire. And very nice indeed, dear boy. You do well—for yourself."

Charley quashed his anger. Too many times he had allowed his father to poison his mood and the moment. "Why have you come up to London? I'm working on a new story and haven't the time for parlor games."

John cut him off with a wave of his gloved hand. "Ah, pardon. The Art God is upon you. I should never have intruded."

Charles swallowed, counted to three. "If this is about money, go home. I have no money to give you."

That threw John Dickens off balance. "What are you saying? Impossible! Dismiss your servants! Surely your own father should come before them!"

Charley leveled at him a finger. "You leave Boodle and Mrs. Plimpton out of this. I give you money each month, and if your wastrel ways have—"

John snickered. " 'Wastrel ways'? Oh, that's really good, Charley. Very literary. It has assonance, alliteration—"

Charley exploded, shouted in a voice to carry across a theater, "I will *Not* stand here and endure insults from a liar!"

Eyes narrowed to slits, John hissed, "Me? The liar? Not even your own wife knows the truth about your family! You'll pay for that, Charles Dickens. No matter how you pretend, you're no better than I. And you'll end up where I did, I promise you!"

The door slowly swung open. Catherine, eyes widened in general alarm, stood in the doorframe. John's personality swung instantly from venomous to virtuous. He strode forward, kissed Mrs. Dickens on the forehead. "Dear daughter, how are you this evening?" John ushered her in, smooth as an anaconda wrapping itself about a kid.

Catherine, the perpetual peacemaker, worried, "I heard voices. You sounded angry . . . "

John patted her hand. "Oh, I am so sorry. I should not have come to this house on money matters even if dire consequences should befall me and I fail a payment and go to . . . " Here John paused dramatically and looked straight at Charley. "Prison!"

"Out, Father, out!" Charley lunged toward his wife to disentangle her from the arms of her in-law. And then it happened, all so swiftly, all so smoothly, that Charley Dickens marveled at his own undoing. There was his father extracting from his wife the offer of money from the clothing allowance while Catherine claimed that such sacrifice brought her joy as all she wanted for her family was peace. Now Catherine was telling Charles to offer John a cigar, or even some cognac, and a nice seat by the fireplace, and would he like to stay?

Dickens, checkmated, could only mutter, "Excuse me, but I have work to do." Then he left the two without a backward glance.

John sighed, shrugged. "Artistic temperament. He was like that as a child."

Catherine looked knowing. "I'm sure you did your best."

John gave her a forced smile, a tight embrace. "Thank you, Catherine, I knew you would understand," he said, looking over her shoulder and into a mirror, the price of which he tried to guess were it brought to a good pawnshop.

That night, fog enshrouded London, bearing with it the rotten scents of the river. Dampness permeated one's pores and clothes, chilling skin, hands, and bones that brandy never quite warmed. Strolling in a mist so thick felt within moments like a shower of cold water. Sensible men did not tarry, resenting the chill and tunnel vision of a London pea-soup fog. They couldn't see where they were going, which heightened their fears of danger.

Not Dickens. He wore a London fog as though it were a cloak of low-lying cloud in which he could ruminate freely, his fast-flowing blood and racing ideas warming him from within.

He followed his feet, aimlessly seeking his way. His father had enraged him, his story had stalled on him. Charles had therefore abandoned both, taking to the streets in a fog of frustration. Never looking beyond the toes of his boots, Charles unwittingly had set a course once he crossed Blackfriars Bridge. A part of his mind knew precisely where his footsteps led. Many times before, many years before, Charley had taken this route.

He found himself within the hour confronting massive gates. He strained to see through the metal bars but caught only snatches of a huge, hulking rock pile of a building. Then he closed his eyes and saw it all. He could envision yard by yard, cell by cell, the inside of this Marshalsea Prison. He knew its interiors and surroundings by heart.

A draft caught and swung the prison's rusting nameplate. It creaked as Charley opened his eyes, the fog breaking before him into misty swatches. From within the prison drifted moans of inmates, curses of turnkeys, the occasional yowl of a maddened dog. He started when a calico cat darted by, clutching in its jaws the squealing prize of a plump and pink-eared rat.

Charley recoiled, looked heavenward, sought any

source of light—a star, the moon, a planet. None shone through the dampened dark. He forced himself to look back through the gates, to the spiked walls and spectral form of this place he hated to death. Without realizing it, he had grasped the railings, in anger as much as need for something solid to which he might cling. His booted feet sank in the mud.

Through barred cell windows, Charley thought he saw some faces of convicts. He knew how they would look up close, these husks of humanity who failed at life—owlish eyes sunk in blood-sapped faces, skin hanging and flapping from lost body fat. They were not men but specimens for zoos, these captives unfit for the freedom they had lost.

Charles sharply sucked in his breath. In the gloom of the uppermost gallery, he thought he saw his father's face—leering, jeering at the workaday world. Charley shook his head hard. He glanced back at the site, but the apparition of his father had fled.

Unnerved, Charley scanned other windows while sights and sounds tumbled chaotically from memory. He could not tell in the fog and dark what was past or present, what images or noises he experienced at the moment and which floated up from childhood times. For one horrific instant he actually saw his own little Charley, face streaked with tears and dirt, staring down from the spot where John Dickens had stood. Charley closed his eyes.

Howling, cackling, clapping. Dickens covered his ears. Pictures, images, people in portals. Himself as a boy staring out the window. A scabied gaoler twisting his arm. His father laughing as he cried out in pain. Tears . . . a scream . . . heartbeat run amok . . . breathing, panting, pulse rate racing. No air, no luck, no light.

Like a geyser, wrath rushed through Charley's veins, erupted in his brain. Incredibly, he heard next a cheery "Yoo-hoo!" Dickens opened his eyes to see a solitary source of light bobbing in the dark. Over it a smiling face peered at the stricken Dickens. "We are closed for the night, sir. You'll have to come back tomorrow!" he explained quite amiably.

In a flash, Dickens returned to the present. He studied the flushed and merry features of a watchguard who bore a torch. How odd that this jovial soul served as gatekeeper to Charley's hell. Dickens then felt his hands before he looked at them; they shook uncontrollably, these hands that mastered blank pages. He knew absolutely the source of these tremors.

Dickens feared that he would some day end up in the Marshalsea, his spirit as a boy imprisoned with those walls, chattel to a past he could not overcome.

Charley said softly to the gatekeeper, "I'll be back," and headed home.

CHAPTER TWO

ithin an hour of awakening, Dickens settled in his den like a grousing bear and scowled as he thumbed through a stack of periodicals. He read aloud to Boodle, who did not even listen. With eyelids at half-mast, the butler might as well have slept.

Brandishing one journal at his manservant, Dickens lamented, "I am hated in the New World for writing <u>American Notes</u>. I must tread more carefully when criticizing the States."

Bewildered, Boodle asked, "States, sir? You are in a state?"

"To be fair, their Edgar Allan Poe writes uncommonly trenchant opinion. I should write to him," Dickens replied.

Boodle tried to be helpful. "And your American friend, uh, Mr. Washboard, was it?"

Dickens glowered. "Washington Irving. And no, we do not communicate. Sadly, some friendships do not withstand certain tests."

"You mean you don't like him?" Boodle sighed.

Dickens shook his head. "Quite the other way around, I fear."

Boodle looked relieved. "Then it's nothing to worry about. Many of your friends don't like you but soon get over it."

Dickens raised an eyebrow. "Thank you, Boodle."

In the cosseted, comfortable world of One Devonshire, Dickens returned to work on his book, trying his best to dismiss sad thoughts about his lost camaraderie with the esteemed Mr. Irving.

While in another world, the pauperized masses of his capital struggled to find mere bread crusts for breakfast. Way to the east and down by the docks, near to the Tower and just up from the water, teemed the hungry, sin-spawning streets of old London.

Here, before the Dark Ages' dawn, the Romans had

encamped at Londinium. Here lay the first limits of a city that had grown downriver to encompass Westminster. Here stood the formidable fortress of the Tower, refuge of kings, stone cage to the condemned. Here lurked the oldest, darkest, bloodiest secrets in London's turbulent history.

The streets were secured by Lucifer's legions. Famished girls lurked in alleyways, sold themselves for food or lodging. Awash in ale, sailors brawled while beggars raided beleaguered vendors. Roger and Paige Knight, partners in crime, led a gang of resourceful thieves, most of them homeless boys. Their clothes didn't fit; none had socks, few shoes. At ebb tide they joined the other mudlarks in scouring the riverbanks for refuse to eat.

Houses here had no chimneys or privies, running water or windows. Horse dung lay in piles on the street. Few denizens ever washed their clothing, and most had not had a bath since birth. Yet up on the roof of one slum dwelling, white poplins and muslins flapped from a line while vats and a wringer lined the railing. At one tub toiled a lady of sixty who scrubbed her laundry in hot, soapy water. Soap was taxed in England, but not in Ireland from which this contraband was smuggled. The laundress herself, Alice McManus, hailed from Armagh. She had ample space in which to wash linens; young Benjamin Newborn fetched her well water.

From a burlap-covered window behind her, Ben called out: "Alice, hurry, before the light is gone."

"Coming, boyo!" Drying her hands on a tea towel, Alice scuttled into a loft where everything looked freshly scrubbed. She had made up two mattresses with clean percale. Washbowls and pitchers sat on painted crates. In one corner stood a sturdy stool and a table made from a ship's pine hatch.

Alice McManus had extended to Ben a living arrangement profitable for them both. She provided lodging and cooked his meals. In return, he fetched well water and taught her to read. It was time now for a spelling lesson. This eve Ben used a copy of <u>The Herald</u> to make their work more interesting.

Alice sat on the stool; Ben knelt beside her. He picked up a pencil and printed W E S T M I N S T E R, then pointed to this word in a headline. Alice frowned. "That's an awful big word, Ben. What's it?"

"You tell me, Alice."

She laughed. "I can't do that!"

"Of course you can. You can spell *king* and *queen* and *prince* and *Peel*. Now, take this word letter by letter." Ben looked deadly serious, his handsome features set hard with resolution.

Alice swallowed, then confronted the mystery word. She struggled with the first three letters for just a few seconds before enunciating accurately, "But it's only West!"

"Good!" Ben ejected. "Go on!" He prodded her until the magic moment when, without hesitation, out came, "Westminster!" Alice's hands flew to her face. Ben grinned. "I told you, Alice. Just take matters a little bit at a time."

She seemed incredulous. "Oh, if me late husband could see this! Me reading. And such a big word, too. Westminster. Tell me again, Ben. Tell me about it."

He spun for her then a tale or two about the splendiferous royal borough, with its beautiful abbey, parks, and palaces and magnificent Parliament House under construction. She was spellbound by the boy. He might as well have told her tales of Xanadu or Timbuktu, so far away and fabled seemed the City's western end.

Love mixed with admiration in the maternal gaze of Alice McManus. Related neither by blood nor by in-laws, Alice and Ben had simply "adopted" each other. So Ben became Alice's "family" in London, just as she was to him his only relative. He would seldom, if ever, speak of his real kin who had somehow or other died disastrously. Alice did not pry or poke into Ben's pain. She just knew with certainty that she would have liked the Newborns. Ben was such a gentle, well-spoken soul and showed such patience with her aching bones. Not many lads aged sixteen would have treated her so kindly. Alice believed that such good graces were heirlooms of the home.

Her smile died hard. It struck her again, that viselike grip on her chest, that sense of suffocation. This time it hit harder than before, closing up her chest, strangling her with phlegm. Her face flushed beet red as she fought for breath. Ben jumped to his feet. "Alice, Alice!

Breathe! Oh, my God. Breathe!" He pounded his fist on her back.

She gasped for air, Ben exhorting her time and again to breathe. "This is the worst!" he said. "We must get your medicine! Where's your payment?"

Between chokes, Alice managed to tell Ben that she hadn't been paid. He then struggled for air. Medicine cost more than they could afford; they needed a nest egg for an emergency like this.

He helped her to her feet. "You'll feel better if you stand, walk around." Feebly she arose and followed Ben about the room. Once her respiration stabilized, Ben dashed to his mattress and snatched from underneath a copy of <u>Bentley's Miscellany</u>. Inside the periodical's front cover lay a precious half-pound note, his last in the world. Ben removed it and hid it in his right shoe. "Don't worry," Ben called out. "I'll be gone for a bit. I won't be long. You'll be right as rain soon enough. I promise you that."

Alice reached under her pillow and pulled out a rosary. "Hurry," she whispered. She grasped the beads and started to pray.

As he left, Ben remembered something. He snatched his wooden crutch propped up against a wall and affected a limp even more severe than the one he actually had.

Posh shops and clubs lined Regent Street, along which Charley Dickens hurried. Punctuality was terribly important to Dickens, although he ran fifteen minutes late for this appointment. For a change, he took no notice of urchins trying to panhandle fine gents on the street. In this neighborhood, beggars demanded discretion, a pushy cadger being bad business for all.

At his club on Pall Mall, the eminent historian Thomas Carlyle fiddled and diddled at his table. Like Dickens, Carlyle suffered from an overly anxious nature. Endowed with the exhausting vitality of the Victorian, Carlyle felt depressingly alive at all times, energetic and melancholic, a truly nettlesome combination.

Suffused with the smug manners and confidence of the servingmen, the dining room seemed an oasis of serenity. Then in bounded Dickens, a spinning top of insecurity, upsetting for a moment the equipoise of the scene. "Thomas!" he called, and dashed right over, muttering apologies to any tables he bumped. His spontaneous joy at seeing Carlyle welled from his deepest being. Dickens felt vindicated by the older man's friendship. Many men of letters disdained Charley's work, yet the stupefyingly learned Carlyle had extended to him the glad hand of fellowship.

Dickens surveyed the table set with rarefied treats. He pounced upon his favorite, maraschino jelly, and instantly slathered this over a scone. Carlyle dutifully asked after Catherine, whose parents he knew quite well. The Hogarths were fixtures in Scottish publishing, well liked and esteemed. Thomas then inquired about the children, heard perfunctory niceties in return. Guessing the direction in which Thomas headed, Charley confirmed that yet another Dickens was on the way.

At that Thomas poised, scone in midair, while Charley ignored his reaction. Shifting to the offensive, Charley asked after Carlyle's work in progress, a massive undertaking on Oliver Cromwell. In truth, Carlyle had bogged down badly in his labors over the bloody Puritan who had seized power in Britain over the beheaded body of his king. The idea of Cromwell troubled Dickens, who couldn't grasp why the genteel Carlyle lionized that monstrous being—cruel, forbidding, unforgiving, a breather of brimstone and husband of the sword.

Cromwell lurked, therefore, as a topic unsettling to them both, so each shifted the conversational brunt back onto his friend. This topical tide flowed back and forth, each dodging a subject he would rather not discuss and fixing on a subject discomfiting to his friend. Finally Thomas cut through the subterfuge.

"Charley, it is I, Thomas Carlyle, confidant, friend, penny-wise Gael. Let us not play games! You are expecting another child, and I suspect you are short of money. Devonshire Terrace is an expensive address, far more so than my own in Chelsea. If you are burdened, say so. I am one to whom you can turn in confidence."

Dickens stiffened. "Is that why you agreed to meet

me today? And are you here not for my benefit but Catherine's?"

Carlyle almost gagged. "Your distrust is ill placed! I am merely being practical. Some people are like that."

Dickens, dashed, tried to quell his disappointment at Carlyle's purpose, which he had, in fact, badly misread. "I appreciate your concern, but it is unnecessary. I am working on a new story and have every confidence that my publishers will render me the assistance I need. Besides, they owe me money."

Carlyle's spirits fell. Dickens had no future in literature, Carlyle knew. The sooner he faced that reality, the better. Certainly some of his early work had sold well, but only as a fleeting fashion in select social herds. Time for truth-telling, no matter how painful. So Thomas Carlyle replied, "Charley, wake up! Humans by nature are blackhearted brutes upon whom you cannot ever depend. Don't expect from your publisher any special treatment."

Charley shot him a glance. "If human beings are such blackhearts, why then should you care about me? Or is it Catherine's welfare that weighs upon your conscience?" Once weighted with moral gravity, Charley's eyes seemed deadly, the barrel end of a pistol aimed in a duel. They cast a heart-stopping darkness, his pupils shrunken to imperceptible specks.

Foiled, Thomas bit his lip. Yes, dammit all, he did

care about this stubborn author of windy hokum . . . and that perpetually fecund wife of his. Yes, Thomas cared very deeply about them both.

Charley, sulking, scraped the last of the jelly from his plate. Silence fell upon their table exquisitely set with Minton china, Sheffield flatware, Baccarat stemware. Prize Regency pieces graced the room while the Chinese carpeting muffled most sound. The liveried waiters silently shuttled about this refuge of wealth and privilege. At the same time, one street scene brought the outer world right to their table.

The two men watched through the window as a carriage stopped at the club. They knew this barouche and four-in-hand of perfectly matched white Hackney horses. The rig belonged to the prime minister, Sir Robert Peel. Before Sir Robert could alight, two mendicant children petitioned the footman, who rudely shooed them away.

Dickens eyed the scene. "He ignores ignorance and want while they cling to me, invade my dreams!"

"Peel's a politician, Charley."

"When he should be a statesman," argued Dickens.

"We don't know much about the man's new party. Give him time." The historian looked warily at his friend.

In the background, the prime minister entered. All eyes swung in his direction. Sir Robert appeared the sort of perfectly patrician man who existed only in the imagination of a court portrait painter. He seemed too august to be entirely a mortal, this titian-haired, blue-eyed fantasy of a Gainsborough. On a cloud of renown, Peel followed the maître d'hôtel to a private dining room, ignoring as he went the many attempts to catch his eye.

Charley tugged at his cravat. "He has joined your club, Thomas?"

Carlyle quickly shot back, "No! I do not know him! Let the man dine in peace."

"He sits on critical legislation that could have helped the mine workers." Dickens tapped the table with sticky fingers.

"Charley, this is no time or place to play the crackpot."

Dickens flared up, "Why not? The disaster in Birmingham should have convinced him. Whole families were lost in that iron mine—women and children along with the men! Unconscionable." Dickens, steaming full speed ahead, leapt to his feet. "I must speak to him straightaway!"

Appalled, Carlyle reached out and grabbed Charley. "Sit, sit, sit! Or I'll have you ejected from my club! It's for gentlemen only!" Dickens hesitated but recovered his manners. He sat. An alarmed Carlyle exhaled and continued, "I told you that you could some day make your feelings known to Parliament. Well, that's why we're here today. You wanted time on the floor of Commons and you've got it. My M.P. will yield you the floor on Wednesday for fifteen minutes—and no more! Now, leave Sir Robert Peel alone."

Charley looked into the hugely intelligent, thoughtful eyes of this righteous man—and calmed himself. Parliament whipped up in Charley such an emotional whirlwind, so critical had he been of that body as a reporter assigned to cover it. Yet he had wanted a chance to take command, if only for the moment, of a stage that had once starred William Pitt and Edmund Burke, Charles James Fox and Daniel O'Connell, orators to weep for and follow. Charles had once been asked to stand for Parliament and at times regretted that he had not done so.

A humbled Charles offered softly, "Thank you, Thomas. I apologize for my behavior just now. I am a crackpot, aren't I?"

Carlyle nodded his assent. "Of course you are! That is your folly and your glory both. Don't ever change. Just learn to solve your own problems afore you take on the woes of the world."

Dickens hesitated. Although Carlyle was right, his words struck hard. Some days, it was easier to change the world than oneself.

Carrying gingerly a brown paper bag, Ben Newborn hobbled from the apothecary shop. From the corner, a street tough observed, a lice-riddled river pirate dressed in slops, straw hat, and guernsey. Once he decided to follow Ben, the sailor exaggerated the swagger in his stride. He knew full well what that lad might carry.

Apothecaries sold all sort of goodies: quinine, pepsin, arsenic. Or maybe those blue pills containing mercury. Henbane. Chloroform. Morphia. Potash, aconite, opium. Yes, opium. That prize justified a wrestling match with a cripple.

The sailor tailed Ben, not knowing that he, in turn, was followed. Roger and Paige Knight, hardened survivors of life on the streets, took an interest in the unfolding scenario. Their names weren't actually Knight but fabrications. Their mother had no surname and had not known their father's. He had vanished years before, signed onto sea and never returned. Their mother had later died in giving birth, leaving Roger and Paige without parents or other family. From that day forward, Roger had looked after Paige.

This little parade halted once the sailor lost Ben down an alleyway. The old salt called out, "I know you're there, lad."

That, Ben was, for he stepped out fearlessly to confront the sailor. "What do you want?" Ben's empty hands gave no clue to the bag or its whereabouts.

"Now, we can be friends, can't we? You and me, lad."

"Why would I want to be friends with you?"

The seasoned sailor, his face disfigured by skin cancers, advanced several paces toward Ben. "I ain't got time for this. Where's that bag you got at the apothecary?"

Ben held his ground. "I stuffed it full of opium and hid it where you'll never know."

This sent the old boy right over the edge. "You little runt! You cain't even fight. Tell me where that bag is — now!"

In the background, Ben watched Paige and Roger approach. Seizing the moment, the sailor lunged toward Ben, who seemed not the slightest bit perturbed. With stunning force, Ben planted his left foot and swung his crutch at his assailant's abdomen. The blow dropped his attacker to the ground. Roger came forward for a closer look. As he did, other gang members trickled into the lane.

The sailor looked to the newcomers for help. "Lads, give me a hand. That li'l faker tried to kill me! You seen him!"

Roger shook his head. "If he wanted to kill you, he would have."

Ben and Roger exchanged glances as the sailor looked about wildly, trapped in a menacing circle of boys. These unwashed, hungry, mean, and angry youths looked at the sailor as though he were dog food. No feeling showed on their jaded faces. They didn't even blink. In a flash, the man scrambled to his feet and made a run for it, shouting over his shoulder, "Don't you touch me, none of you!"

An unscrubbed six-year-old said in awe, "Look at that! Ben's got shoes!"

"Two of 'em, too!" another waif exclaimed.

Roger jerked his head. "Git, all of you. I want to talk

to Ben." Muttering amongst themselves, they sauntered off, Paige catcalling in a resentful voice. "Our carriage has arrived! Pardon us, Master Newborn!"

Roger asked simply, "Alice sick again?" He was full-grown at seventeen and burly for any age. He might have been taller, but rickets bowed his legs. His reddened gums ruined a potentially winning smile. His black eyes gleamed, but whether from fever or ill temper, no one quite knew.

Roger didn't wait for an answer. "Listen, when Alice be gone, come back, Ben. Who else you got but us?"

Ben shook his head vigorously. "Alice is not going to die."

Roger sighed. "Sure. Like you got the money to keep buying her medicine. Why not hire a surgeon?"

Ben retrieved from a cranny in the wall his precious brown paper bag. Without another word, he headed for the street. Roger wouldn't give up. "Ben, you could earn a real living with us. We can use you. What's holding you back?"

Ben paused, spoke carefully so as not to insult Roger. "I have to do things my own way. Some day I'll pay you back. You have my word on that. When I first came to London and knew not a soul, had nowhere to go, you helped me. I might have starved to death, or frozen, if it hadn't been for you, but I've got to do things in my own way, and thieving isn't it."

Roger stared critically at the well-spoken boy from

Birmingham, then shook his head. "You turn that head of yours to thievin' and ain't nobody in London could beat the two of us. Class and cash. That's you and me."

Ben smiled and turned away.

Jack interjected, "You could get Alice to a medical man."

Ben hesitated on the bleak little street. His temples throbbed, aching from the pain of lost opportunity. He knew that he would never escape from this life of poverty, drudgery, or beggary, scrapping for food, medicine, and love. It really made more sense for him to team up with Roger, yet Ben could not abandon Alice . . . or himself. In him flowed a force he could not name, one that came to him in deepest sleep and left his godforsaken soul renewed, fortified for life. This mysterious wellspring in Ben's inner being pulled him away from a life of crime and therefore Roger Knight. Toward what, though, he did not know.

Still, Ben liked Roger and felt obliged to say, "Careful. Peel's putting plainclothes in Whitechapel. You could get nabbed. If you're nabbed, you'll be hung."

Roger, arms akimbo, guffawed, then spat on the ground. "Where'd you hear that?"

Ben bit his cheek in exasperation. "I mean it, Roger. I read it in <u>The Herald</u>. Take it seriously, would you?"

Roger stopped slouching and pulled himself erect. "Hell's bells, he is. They be no police he puts on our streets, just spies to keep us from riotin' again or mixin' up matters. His bobbies protect the rich. Ain't no rich in Whitechapel, believe me."

Roger stormed off, infuriated, as were many of the poor, by the idea of the "bobbies," policemen nicknamed for Robert Peel. With the other's back turned toward him, Ben discerned a slice of steel glinting from Roger's belt. A blade. A handle.

A dagger.

CHAPTER THREE

t was the morning of his going to the great House of Commons, and Charley Dickens could scarcely check his stride. He set a blistering pace from Regent's Park to the river, his spirits seeming to soar higher than the pigeons of St. Paul's. He had just a few minutes to make his views known, but he enjoyed every confidence that the

ministers would receive his message. Yes, this was the sort of glorious morn that made a soul glad to be alive, to be on a mission, to be, thank God, British.

Across the Thames, smokestacks spewed foul odors and fumes. The river itself hardly flowed. Caked sewage and trash floated idly by, the Thames an outhouse for a city of running sewers. On a cool day such as this, however, the river's rank odors didn't carry too far and shouldn't worsen the displaced Parliament's mood.

Nine years earlier, the building itself had burned to the ground, leaving the nation's ministers without a proper place to meet. They convened for the nonce in quarters cramped and dank, windows shut and shaded against contagion. This made the chamber unnaturally dark and a poor place in which to read or write. Neither did it help that political parties were aboil with argument and at last count, a half dozen parties were sitting.

It was a house divided against itself—one side attired in sartorial glory while the other wore rough-hewn fibers that scratched and smelled and often clashed. The well-heeled Tories and Conservatives seemed masters of themselves, chatting in low tones and exchanging wry smiles. At the opposite end of the social scale, Liberals— really the conservatives of the defunct Whig party— popped up and down like jacks-in-the-box, glad-handing and whispering, scuttling back and forth, wearing worried looks and rubbing themselves. A handful of Radicals skulked in the back, hatching plots for such unthinkable

schemes as the secret ballot and votes for adult males —
all of them.

Thomas Carlyle and Charles Dickens studied the
scene. Outside in the corridors, devotees of the latter
milled and gossiped, rhapsodized and cooed, tried to gain
entry but were turned away. Dickens attracted women
enamored of his beauty, his compassion for the poor, his
whiplash wit. More than the ladies, Dickens avoided
critics or students stalking the hall, those men of Fleet
Street and Oxbridge who disdained his work as an insult
to letters. Still, Charles felt flattered that they had come
at all. Only yesterday had the handbills and tabloids cir-
culated with Charley's name listed as special speaker to
Commons. Surely this turnout spoke of his enduring
popularity.

Charles fretted like a foxhound straining at his leash,
wishing to get on with the Chase. This unsettled Carlyle.
He worried that Dickens might lose his self-restraint or
expect too much of these harried ministers.

The one unruffled minister on the floor was Sir
Robert Peel. To Carlyle, the prime minister looked bored
by these petty doings of lesser men. In truth, Peel came
not from the nobility but from a family of upstarts. His
father had owned cotton mills in the Midlands, infamous
enterprises that exploited child labor. Yet the son had
earned considerable respect as a lucid speaker and deft
legislator. Of late he had formed his Conservative party,
breaking with Tories and finding his own way. Where he

would take the rest of England, no one knew. Peel gave no hint with his glassy-eyed gaze and fugitive smile.

Carlyle's eyes roamed to the small Strangers' Gallery where a lucky handful had wangled seats. Without intending to, he settled his searching eyes upon an intense-looking lad of perhaps fifteen or sixteen years of age. Carlyle's brows contracted in curiosity. This boy, dressed in raggedy clothing, read aloud from a magazine to the well-dressed but wizened gent on his left. The remarkable tableau fixed Carlyle's attention.

Sensing that he was being watched, the boy suddenly turned his eyes on Carlyle. So smoothly, so assuredly did Benjamin Newborn stare back at Carlyle that the latter felt unnerved. Abashed, the man smiled and looked away. At that instant all heard the sergeant at arms herald: "Mr. Charles Dickens!" followed by the Speaker of the House trumpeting to no avail: "Order! Order!" The gallery had erupted in applause. "Order! Order!" The Speaker again shouted, trying gamely to gavel the ragtag group to silence.

The limelight fell on Dickens, the target of every Tory, Conservative, Liberal, Radical, Scot, Irish Nationalist, and Welshman in the House. All glowered at the uppity intruder. Charles felt a momentary spasm of stage fright. Alarmed, he grabbed Carlyle by the elbow. "What if they hate me, Thomas?"

Thomas Carlyle forced a chuckle. "Heavens, there's

nothing here to fear except yourself. Just hold your temper, Charley."

At that, Dickens grimaced . . . and strode to the dais.

In the five minutes since Dickens had started speaking, Carlyle felt perspiration pool in parts of his body no Victorian gentleman would ever name. He was miserable, truly, this greater outdoorsman who thrived on country air and fresh sea breezes. The scene, by contrast, animated Dickens, who drank up attention as though it were oxygen.

He did cut a dashing figure, as romantic-looking as Byron off on a crusade or Shelley in requited love. Having taken fleeting turns onstage, he knew very well how to rivet his listeners. All the way to the back of the gallery, ears were attuned like spaniels to their masters. He spoke to them slowly, distinctly, hiding a hiss with which he pronounced the letter *s*. This embarrassing defect sometimes sounded like a lisp.

" . . . Nor do I believe that the working classes are the devious rogues that the educated would have us believe. This I do believe: that the first blessing of self-improvement is self-respect, an inward dignity of character which not even the direst poverty can vanquish. Let the downtrodden chase from their hearths the demons of ignorance, and self-respect, even hope, are left them!"

While spectators in the gallery beamed their approval at these magnanimous words, Tory ministers vented their disdain. Within earshot of Dickens, one cackled to the other, "What's left him are his senses."

Dickens gave no hint of having heard the M.P. Quite calmly he continued, "I read recently of one child, six years old, who has been twice as many times in the hands of the police as years have passed over his head. These are the eggs from which gaolbirds are hatched."

This time the Tory catcalled, "Who hatched you?" Titters floated from that side of the floor, but Dickens ignored the opposition. Carlyle checked his watch. His friend had five minutes left.

Dickens paused a moment before speaking again, imbuing with measured gravity his carefully chosen words: "It is incumbent upon the lawmakers of a truly civilized people to free its citizens from the slavery of ignorance. Ignorance is the despairing parent of misery and crime."

This brought the Tory to his feet, a chore for a man whose overstuffed belly bobbled as he stood. "Do I understand you correctly, Mr. Dickens? You would demand that your government promote education for everybody? Build schools for the laboring classes?"

Dickens took on the Tory. "Nothing less may give us the civil society that our United Kingdom deserves."

Carlyle tried to read the prime minister's reaction and

found none. The historian clucked his tongue at Peel's apparent apathy. Few knew that Sir Robert had survived a hunting accident in which an experimental cartridge had exploded like shrapnel. Due to a severe hearing loss and continual buzz in his head, neither of which he ever discussed, Peel was wrongly judged by many. His upper-crust indifference merely shielded his maladies.

Murmurs of approval, mutters of dissent, brought Carlyle back to the scene. Surprisingly, the Tory next smiled, announcing as though he really didn't care, "What the poor deserve, I can't even mention in polite society." Ministers on the front benches laughed their assent, which thoroughly irked Dickens. Feigning incredulity, he asked, "*Parliament* is polite society?"

Hoots and shouts sailed from the gallery while a half dozen ministers hissed and booed. Carlyle held his head, which ached hideously, and wished that he were home. Another Tory, looking unscathed by the fracas, arose and commented coolly, "What you propose, Mr. Dickens, would undermine the very social structures upon which our Crown and country repose. I have a name for that, sir: treason!"

"Hear! Hear" called half the floor in approval of the Tory's words. Naysayers in the gallery, however, also made themselves heard as Dickens gathered his wits. Carlyle hated the whole business. Treason? Poppycock. The progressive young Queen Victoria had recently wed the open-minded Prince Albert. So the Tory was obviously baiting Dickens to say something truly infamous. At that thought, Carlyle actually felt a chill.

Dickens had little left to his mental fuse. "For any minister who believes that a society can codify injustice and still call itself civilized, I have a name: common. What we need to unite this kingdom is a house of uncommon men." With that, he slammed the rostrum with his fist.

Whooping its delight, the gallery rose as one to its feet, led by Benjamin Newborn. The young man goaded onlookers into raucous applause and resounding shouts of "Hear! Hear!" The Speaker shouted right back: "Order! Order!" but any hope of order died in all the ruckus.

The Tory minister's fuse, too, was lit, and any semblance of his reserve died hard. He fairly shrieked: "Mr. Speaker! Shall we suffer insult from this man who abuses the platform we have, as a special honor, provided him today?"

Too late. Dickens lost his temper, leveling a finger at the angry M.P. and retorting with words he fairly spit out: "My platform comes from a people whose best interests you represent. Abuse their trust, sir, and you lose your standing."

Carlyle covered his eyes. He had warned Dickens about taking bait. Now fifty ministers spat invective at Charley, who shouted right back and pounded the platform. It was a melee, the gallery heartily joining the fray. Some observers lobbed unidentifiable objects from the balcony while the Speaker hurled pointless threats in return. The din rose steadily higher and louder, with no sign of a truce anywhere in sight.

Realizing that he had lost control of the situation and invited not agreement but contempt for his ideas, Charley looked shaken and lost. How the great William Pitt had handled such people, not even Charles Dickens could imagine.

Unnoticed and without fanfare, one tatterdemalion minister stood. Unlike the elegantly attired men on the opposite benches, this red-faced fellow wore a thread-bare coat and boots that had never seen polish or wax. He simply waited, gnarled hands clasped across his breast. In orotund Welsh tones, he quietly intoned again and again: "Mr. Speaker . . . Mr. Speaker."

It worked, though no one knew why. This sadly clad man, compelling for the dignity in his humble bearing, settled the House as the sergeant at arms could not. Voices fell, people sat, embarrassed by their barbarous behavior. The Welshman cleared his throat, calmly let his words flow forth. "With due respect to you, Mr. Speaker, and to you, Mr. Prime Minister . . . I mean, Sir Robert . . . I has a few words to say."

A few Tories groaned, but most affected respect and welcomed the chance to sit again. Said one to the other, "Oh, joy. Wisdom from the Great Unwashed."

The farmer-minister from the mountains of Snow-donia continued, "Mr. Dickens, yer a fine man, I don't doubt. And you, Sir Robert, I knows you be an Oxford man and learnt what I'll never know in me life, of thinkers and scholars and kings whatnot. All I know is cows and sheep and mebbe a tale of King Arthur or two. I'm a poor man from a poor district. I learnt to read only afore a-coming to this House."

Minds immediately started to wander; a snore or two wafted from back benches. In contrast, Dickens appeared enchanted, fascinated by this unpretentious man who won his undivided attention. What came next, however, rattled the author.

"Mr. Dickens," the Welshman said softly, "look at yer fine clothes, yer hair, yer hands. What do you know of bein' poor?"

Dickens looked as though he had just been struck, his expression one of betrayal. This surprised Carlyle, who watched as Charley's jaw slackened, as he struggled but failed to find any words.

The Welshman politely advised, "Go home, Mr. Dickens. We of the workin' poor can fight our own battles, thank you."

The farmer sat to polite applause from the Tories across the floor. This fellow whose name was no doubt unpronounceable, and was probably spelled with all sorts of consonants and no vowels, had just put Charles John Huffam Dickens in his place. Bravo. Pip, pip.

To the surprise of all gathered, be they friend or foe, pauper or Tory, knight or ex-Whig, Charley Dickens picked up his papers and walked away from Commons. He had surrendered.

As he departed, Prime Minister Sir Robert Peel looked after him.

On the street, Benjamin Newborn loitered.

The lad espied Dickens and Carlyle struggling through a small knot of admirers, nearly all of them female. To Ben, Dickens cut a romantic and restless figure while Thomas Carlyle seemed merely nerve-wracked. The taller and older of the two, Carlyle appeared at age forty-eight almost a fatherly figure to Dickens, whose dapperness made him look even younger.

Ben, too, felt nerve-wracked. He stood a mere three meters away from a man he truly revered. Certainly he couldn't just dawdle like an idiot and let the moment pass. Ben's side vision then ensnared what he definitely did not wish to see. Ambling toward Dickens was Paige Knight, pickpocket extraordinaire. Ben tried to catch Paige's eye but was studiously ignored.

As Dickens signed autographs, Carlyle's attention wandered to the sight of Ben Newborn. There was that lad from the Strangers' Gallery, the one who had read aloud from his magazine and later led the applause in support of Charles Dickens. Now Carlyle could see up close just what manner of boy he might be.

The lad's high cheekbones gave his hazel eyes a lupine look, as though he were a timber wolf scanning the forest. A thatch of blond hair fell over his brow, partially obscuring entrancing eyes, bold and shy in turns. His hard-set mouth and strained neck muscles indicated riptides of buried feeling.

Difficult to gauge were his height and physique as Ben came forward on a homemade crutch. The sight made Carlyle frown. So did the silly prattle he could not help but overhear. One young lady told Dickens how much she loved his speech even though she hadn't heard any of it but was stranded the entire time in the corridor. The other young lady raved that Pickwick Papers remained her favorite. That follows, thought Caryle. Pickwick was trash.

Ben hurried as he saw Paige sidle up behind Dickens. From several steps away, Ben called out: "Mr. Dickens! Can you tell me the time?"

The question startled Charley. He stopped, shrugged, and pulled from his pocket a magnificent white-gold watch. "It's half four, young man." As Dickens did this, Paige turned and glowered at Ben. Foiled by the interloper, the pickpocket would nab no booty from Dickens.

Summoning the rest of his nerve, Ben approached his idol. One maiden prated, "Now here is a fine illustration of your point, Mr. Dickens. We stand not far from a clock tower, but this illiterate soul cannot tell us what the hour is. Yet with the proper schooling—"

Ben interrupted by proffering a sadly battered copy of <u>Bentley's Miscellany</u>. Very evenly he asked Mr. Dickens, "Please, sir, would you sign this installment of <u>Oliver Twist</u>? I did enjoy the story, but why do your evil characters fascinate more than the good? I mean, who wouldn't find the thieving Fagin more intriguin' than Oliver, who can be such a simp?" Benjamin looked at the fawning female as though she were a charlady clad in rags and ashes. She recoiled.

The others fell silent. Carlyle tugged at his cravat. The ladies stared at the intruder as though a little green man from Mars had come to Westminster. They fanned themselves with their lace handkerchiefs and waited for the explosive Dickens to reply. Dickens took his time, too.

"You know my name, young man, but I know not yours. You take unfair advantage. Introduce yourself."

Gathering himself, the boy seemed to grow an inch in height. "I am Benjamin James Newborn, sir, but known to my friends as Ben."

Dickens extended his gloved hand for a shake. "My friends call me Charley. You may call me Mister." Ben flinched at the rebuke, then noted that Dickens smiled at him. In return, Ben shyly offered his surprisingly smooth right hand. With real vigor, Dickens shook it, an act that astonished Benjamin. He hardly heard Dickens say, "I'm impressed, I admit. I've always believed illiteracy to be the true prison of the poor, but you have found the key to freedom. Not only have you read my work, you have expressed rather freely your critical opinion. Do you still wish that I sign your magazine?"

Undone by the gift of a handshake from Dickens, Ben could only croak, "Oh, sir, would you?"

"Gladly." So Dickens scribbled his name in pencil on the very first page of the periodical. "What ho!" he then called. "Our noncommittal prime minister!" All turned to see Peel exit Parliament. Dickens exploited the moment. He pulled from a pocket his calling card and slipped this inside Ben's magazine. At the same time, Peel's luxurious coach stopped at the curb where the prime minister waited.

Dickens handed the magazine back to Ben. "Master Newborn, I've given you my card. If you wish, leave word with my publishers and we'll discuss the matter of a crutch. A bad one can worsen a limp. Now, if you will excuse me, I have things to say to our fence-straddling P.M.!"

With that, the father of <u>Oliver Twist</u> dashed off, flailing his cane. Carlyle cringed. He hoped that Charles wouldn't catch up to the carriage and pinion the lordly P.M.

At the same time, Ben held his magazine as though it were the Holy Grail, a vessel of holy, life-giving belief. The young ladies, handerkerchiefs shielding their noses, melted into the crowd.

Carlyle, knowing not what to make of the boy, attempted conversation. "I don't suppose you've read our Walter Scott."

Without looking up, Ben replied, "<u>Ivanhoe</u>? <u>The Bride of Lammermoor</u>? <u>Guy Mannering</u>?"

Carlyle smiled gamely. "I thought so." He could not know that Ben hadn't actually read all those books. Then again, much of literary London had never read Scott cover to cover — or Thomas Carlyle, for that matter.

Thomas watched Dickens chase after Peel's barouche, which pulled into a traffic jam of carriages. Meanwhile, Carlyle felt abandoned to this insolent urchin whose eyes smoldered like branding irons. He needn't have fretted.

His idol gone, Ben departed — under the steady glare of Paige Knight. In afterthought, he stopped and called out to Carlyle, "I like that you write histories of heroic men. That's very important, I think." Then off he hobbled.

Carlyle was amazed by the magnitude of his gratitude for this entirely offhand compliment, come not from an Oxford don or fellow of the Royal Academy. He couldn't even explain why it felt so wonderful that Benjamin Newborn should approve of him.

CHAPTER FOUR

n ancient and fabled highway, the Strand linked the City of London with the royal borough of Westminster. First paved by Richard Lion-Heart, the Strand had been busy ever since. No longer lined by meadows, the thoroughfare hosted thriving businesses leading toward the Thames. In its midst reposed a sweet little church,

St. Mary's-le-Strand, the second so named to inhabit the spot. The first had been pulled down long ago by the King's Protector, the duke of Somerset. The duke had promised to build another church but was fatally foiled when he was beheaded instead. In the second church eventually erected, John Dickens had married Elizabeth Barrow, the mother of Charley Dickens.

On this historic, colorful, pageant-filled passage operated Charley's publisher: Ledrook and Squib, No. 186. Rufus Ledrook seemed a droopy old soul with the physique of a domestic turkey complete with wattled red neck. Josiah Squib, by contrast, appeared rather hawkish with his piercing eyes, overgrown nose, and arms that flapped in agitation. Both listened to Charles hold forth before Rufus arose, left this sales pitch to his partner. In business together for about ten years, Rufus handled the money, Josiah the artists. Negotiations with woolly-headed writers, Ledrook delegated to Squib.

Squib had given careful consideration to Charley's request for royalties and an advance. However, given his first opportunity, Squib dropped onto a desk in front of Dickens a series of hardbound books: <u>Pickwick Papers</u>, <u>The Old Curiosity Shop</u>, <u>Oliver Twist</u>, <u>Nicholas Nickleby</u>. He said rather quietly, "There is one problem, Charles, with all of them. They don't sell. They haven't sold in a year. They are dead. Charley, you're dead to begin with. There is no doubt whatsoever."

These words struck Charley's heart as hammerblows. His brow furrowed from disbelief. "Surely there's been some mistake—a bookkeeping error. How can there be no royalties or earnings from such a collection?"

Squib shook his head. "No, no, no. The public, it seems, no longer craves your opinion on matters immortal and weighty."

Charley, trying hard to regain his composure, offered, "If that were true, Josiah, why was I invited to speak to Commons?"

"Pardon me for saying so, but I heard that your speech wasn't exactly a bull's-eye. Oh, your votaries still follow you, but do half of them read you? Certainly they're not buying you. As for Parliament, well, I doubt that you won any converts to your cause. Heavens, the ministers can't win converts to their own causes, and a successful outsider would just threaten them all. They'd join forces against you." Squib smiled congenially and twiddled his thumbs.

These revelations from Squib rattled Dickens to the marrow of his bones. When distrustful or frightened, Dickens avoided eye contact and so he stood to one side, vision fixed on the floor. Seeing this, the publisher reinforced his points. "Charles, you are free to examine our records. All I ask is that you consider the possibility that you have exhausted the wellsprings of your creative mind. It is no more knotty a problem than that. You can always return to journalism, you know. You had a reputation. And didn't you tell me you'd joined Middle Bar with the thought of becoming a lawyer?"

Dickens walked in a semicircle, counting nails in the floor's wooden slats. He argued, "Yes, yes, I know I said all that, but you must hear me out. I know this new story is a marked improvement over anything else I've done. It will revive the others, you'll see. Didn't my works earn you money in the past? Granted, their lives were short, but they burst upon the scene netting you profits. True?"

Squib nodded. "That I cannot deny. You were only half dead at the time."

Locked onto his goal, Charles ignored the gibe. "One advance, Josiah, and you'll see those profits again. Just one more time!" He fixed his soul-piercing gaze on his publisher.

Squib swallowed, summoning his nerve. "Charles, you fell out with the first publisher of <u>Oliver Twist</u>, you never finished another novel you promised that publisher, and your famous illustrator of <u>Pickwick Papers</u> committed suicide. Have you ever stopped to think that it might be you?"

This ghastly litany disturbed Josiah Squib. As much as he had given up on Dickens, it was always sad to see a galvanic man prostrate with need and bad luck. Besides, Charley's luck might turn and the next work deliver handsomely. So Josiah conceded on second thought. "However, we could advance a modest sum should your story promise solid sales. If it sells poorly in serial form, we would quit for good each other's professional company. You go somewhere else, agreed?"

At that instant Charles thought not of the future but only of the present. Certainly there were other publishers, but he hadn't the time to hunt one down. His lull in sales wouldn't help, either. What he needed, what mattered at that very moment, was the man who stood before him: Josiah Squib. Thus he exclaimed, "Agreed! You will never regret that you fostered this new work. I am confident it will stand as my monument."

"Spare me, Charles. London is chockablock with monuments. Just pray that your new book sells. By the way, what is the title of this godsend to letters?"

"Titles?" Dickens fudged.

"Yes," said Squib, "that name by which a book is known. What you call it. What a printer stamps on its spine."

Dickens paused. "Oh, that. It's called <u>Martin</u> . . . <u>Chuzzlewit</u>!"

Squib mulled this news. In truth, he disliked the name, but grinning as broadly as a crescent moon, he crooned, "Sounds like a seller to me!"

Dickens, flowers in hand, bounded up the steps to One Devonshire Terrace. Charging through the door, he ran right into a gaggle of offspring whom he managed to embrace all at once. Catherine strode down the steps and looked, in pitiful expectation, at her spouse. He nodded at her—yes! The lady grabbed the balustrade as relief surged through her burdened body.

Dickens concealed the bad news lest that threaten Catherine's condition. He informed her of the <u>Chuzzlewit</u> advance but not of the failure of his other books. Instead, he believed that his new story's success would rekindle public interest in the others. The Dickens family would soon, and safely, pass through the straits that threatened them now.

The next several weeks ground by with hard labor and high expectation. Charles, living virtually incommunicado, penned furiously the <u>Chuzzlewit</u> episodes. His handwritten scrips turned into folios that were bound into periodicals and hawked about town. These installments even reached Ben Newborn's loft where he read them aloud to Alice.

One day Dickens toiled at his desk without noticing that Boodle had entered. Boodle moaned. Dickens looked up—yes? he asked without uttering a word.

Boodle held up a newspaper neatly folded in four. Across one quadrant was emblazoned the headline: CHUZZLEWIT A FIZZLEWIT! Boodle carried under his other arm a half dozen papers bearing the same bad news.

Dickens did not even blink. He stared at the headline. Blood drained from his head with the onset of shock. Slowly he arose, uncomprehending, his feet disconnected to the rest of his body as he tried to find his direction. He walked as far as the divan and sat, eyes boring into the carpet. He had not for an instant contemplated the likelihood that <u>Chuzzlewit</u> might fail, so pleased he was with the maturation of his writing in the piece. Now he considered the worst possiblity of all, that he had fooled, even deluded himself, that he had lost his capacity to intuit the truth. His powers had deceived him.

Boodle slowly shut the door to the garden. The front doorbell rang. Catherine answered and saw on the stoop a dispirited Thomas Carlyle. By the anxiety etched in Catherine's features, he knew that she had seen the papers. So had he. "May I enter?" he asked, feeling silly for being so obvious.

"Oh, please, Thomas. It's good to see you!" said Catherine, welcoming rescue.

Thomas handed his hat and cane to Boodle, then followed Catherine into the drawing room. Just before the door closed behind them, Boodle heard his mistress say, "I don't know what to do!"

The butler stood lost in the hallway as Dickens brushed by without comment. He did not join the others in the drawing room but grabbed his hat, cane, and gloves and hurried outdoors. Boodle looked from one door to the next. The hall clock bonged . . . and did not stop.

Twilight yielded to the cold snap of night as Dickens arrived at MacPherson's Pawn Shop. He approached the establishment on Goodge Street and stopped, his eyes skimming the storefront's signs. He bit deeply his lower lip before pulling from his fob the golden watch. He held this white-gold treasure, the keeper of his times, then strode through the entrance to MacPherson's.

Dickens did not know it, but he had been followed. Across the street lurked a shadowy figure who waited until Dickens left ten minutes later. Another half hour passed until MacPherson shut up shop. The wary adolescent studied security measures taken by the owner—removing merchandise from windows, lowering and locking gratings, double-bolting front and side doors.

It was a curious, bemused, calculating Paige Knight who witnessed this moment of ignominy for Charley. Paige strolled away, singing softly, "When will you pay me, say the bells of Old Bailey? When I get rich, say the bells of Shoreditch!"

Suppers at One Devonshire had grown gloomy and lifeless, so much so that the children noticed. Dickens stared vacantly, mesmerized by a candle flame. Little Charley offered, "Papa, you haven't done any magic tricks for us in a long, long time."

Dickens explained absentmindedly, "Sorry. I was writing a book."

"That's not magic!" Mamie challenged.

Dickens smiled ruefully. "You're right, darling. It wasn't."

Catherine brightened. "Charles, why don't you stage a magic show? It would be good for us all."

Mamie cheered instantly, "Oh, Papa, please. I want the Traveling Doll!"

Her brother argued, "I want the Flying Money!"

Catherine interrupted, "Money already flies through the house. What about the Pudding Wonder?"

At that suggestion, all the children chimed in. They loved the Pudding Wonder best of all. Dickens had staged these magic shows ever since the arrival of little Charley. The firstborn Dickens infant had come into the world on January 6, Epiphany, the feast of the Magi or Wise Men. The day before, January 5, ended Twelfth Night — that ancient festival spanning the days from Christmas to Epiphany. This season was therefore especially dear to Charles as he associated it with the miracle of birth, new life, his babies fresh from God.

Charley muttered, but with a smile on his face, "Why not? It's all I'm good for anymore . . . parlor tricks!" He never ceased to be flattered by his children's glee in his performances.

The children ran to the drawing room, Mamie fetching from the hallway her father's top hat. For a moment Catherine and Charley sat alone, seated at opposite ends of the table. Each wondered how long they could continue as they were, with yet another child on the way.

Dickens did not look at her as he said without expression, "I'm dining next week at Middle Temple."

Catherine shut her eyes. "You'll make a wonderful barrister, Charles."

In the drawing room, the children dragged chairs into a semicircle. Catherine entered and took her place while Boodle and Mrs. Plimpton stood in back. Charley and Mamie also sat while Katey, unnoticed, toddled into the hall.

For a few brief, fleeting minutes, Charley Dickens could forget his woes. With dramatic flourishes, he launched into his act, showing his rapt audience the inside and out of an empty saucepan. Then one, two, he waved his hand back and forth across the pan and — voilà! Out came a delectable plum pudding!

Dickens gestured to Boodle, who came forward with the top hat turned upside down. "Now," said Dickens, "my plum pudding is never complete without some heat to tastify my treat. So here, dear friends . . . "

With a sweeping motion, Dickens passed the pudding over the hat, whereupon an orange flame shot up, nearly toppling Boodle. The children squealed as Dickens warmed the dessert over the flame. Catherine applauded. "You've not lost your touch, Charles!"

"Nor my appetite," he replied.

It never failed. The Pudding Wonder always made them laugh even though they knew what was coming and had never figured it out.

Mrs. Plimpton carried the pudding to the sideboard

where she had set the dessert forks and dishes. Charley and Mamie, grand inquisitors of their magical father, vied for his attention. They demanded to know his secrets, which, of course, he never divulged. He smiled, and joked, and jostled his children, none of whom sensed that he was at the very same time wrestling with a black, bottomless anguish so terrible, not even Catherine guessed it. His soul had stumbled onto the quicksand of despair.

Without warning or preamble, Charley heard Catherine scream. The baby! In terror, he called out, "What is it! Catherine, what is it!" His wife never panicked. Something terrible must have happened.

Catherine flew to the doorway which framed tiny Katey. The child had stuffed into her mouth some manuscript pages while other leaves littered the hall.

Catherine scooped up her toddler and tugged from her mouth a gooey wad. Mrs. Plimpton scooted about the floor, grumbling as she gathered papers.

Appalled, Catherine solemnly informed her husband, "Katey has eaten Cromwell."

This, Dickens did not need to hear. Surely this could not be the one and only copy of Cromwell which Dickens had begged Carlyle for days to lend him. This precious, priceless manuscript could not have been consumed in part by an infant. All London knew the horror story of Carlyle's manuscript for <u>The French Revolution</u>. John

Stuart Mill's maid had used it to light a fire. Now Katey had used another work as a pacifier. The Dickens family would never live this down.

Charley scrambled about the floor, helping Mrs. Plimpton collect the wreckage. This turn of events sickened him. He bemoaned, "If this is the only copy, Cromwell himself shall come to haunt us."

Mamie screamed . . . "No, no, no! He's going to haunt us!"

"Oh, quiet," said her five-year-old brother. You don't even know who Cromwell is. Papa, who is he?"

Dickens resorted to a theatrical tone, imbuing their plight with the melodramatic as he explained to his little children, "He was the man who stole Christmas! He stole all of it, the holly and the ivy, the Yule log and the miracle play, the mistletoe and merriment, and even plum pudding! He banished it all as papist flummery unfit for the Puritan soul!"

Little Charley gulped, "Is he coming to haunt us?"

Mamie sobbed as her father responded. "Would it make any difference? What's another ghost in the story of my life?"

"Charles!" Catherine sharply admonished him. "Darling, Daddy was only teasing."

Dickens stood. "No, Daddy wasn't. Oliver Cromwell was a mean, nasty, bloodthirsty man who killed all the fun and almost all the Irish. He bore a grudge against life and that's why he's a ghost, stalking people who just want to live and be happy at least twice before they die!"

As Charley's level of ire rose quickly, Catherine wisely shooed the children off to bed. Mamie proved inconsolable. "He stole Christmas and he's coming to haunt us!" Katey, not comprehending any of this, screamed to show solidarity with her sister.

Little Charley looked back down the stairs. "Papa, could we have a Christmas like the one in the story you read us, the one about Christmas from long ago? Papa, please. Why don't you bring back a *real* Christmas?"

Charles glowered. "I don't know what you mean."

Catherine shot her husband a look. "You know those wonderful tales of Mr. Irving's."

"Oh, that!" Charles shrugged. "His were passable passages."

Catherine drew herself up and stood her ground. "Charles John Huffam Dickens. You loved them! You said so at the time." Catherine rarely scolded her husband. The children loitered, awaiting results of this skirmish.

Dickens lowered his voice as he said to his wife, "Have you forgotten? Mr. Irving and I aren't even speaking!"

"Isn't Christmas about opening one's heart?" Catherine's stubborn Scottish blood had finally come to the fore.

Mamie poked her face through the balustrade. "Would Christmas scare Crumwall away?"

Mrs. Plimpton added, "Wouldn't it be grand! A real

English country Christmas, come home to London at last! And all these years after Cromwell killed it!"

Mamie jumped up and down. "Papa, please!"

At that instant the slow, heavy, methodical banging of a brass knocker thundered from the green front door. The children shrieked: "Cromwell!" and ran upstairs.

Muttered Dickens as he answered the door, "The whole ruddy family is balmy."

On the stoop stood Bartholomew Bane, pallid, emaciated, fish-eyed. Taken aback by seeing his banker at the door, Dickens asked, "Bartholomew, what brings you out at this hour?"

When Bartholomew smiled, his eyes disappeared. When he spoke, his rasping voice gave way to shallow coughs which he suppressed by applying two bony fingers to his lips. "Good evening, Mr. Dickens. Good evening, Mrs. Dickens. Would you be so kind as to spare me (cough, cough) a moment?"

Catherine nodded and gestured toward the drawing room. There Mr. and Mrs. Dickens proceeded while Bane seemed to float above ground, his shoes concealed under his great black cape. Dickens closed the door behind them.

Giving the room a frank appraisal, the banker began, "With heartfelt regrets, I am here to tell you what the bank has decided it must on the morrow do. I must, I fear (cough, cough), demand your eviction from this house."

"What! That can't be!" exclaimed Catherine. Dickens could not even reply, feeling felled as a tree in the forest by this blow.

Bane gave a sigh calculated to sound sympathetic. "Your house payments are — oh, forgive me for saying it, dastardly lot into which fate has cast me — long overdue and too often overdue. Therefore, our board of directors, after careful consideration, has elected to take possession. I naturally (cough, cough) resisted this course of action with the full force of my will and unblemished name."

Dickens responded dully, "We made a payment only last month."

"Ah, but that was for August. This is, I dare say it, October." Bane fluttered his eyelashes in mock apology as he looked back and forth at the two.

Unarmed with any ideas, Dickens remained rooted to the spot as he heard from his banker, "Barring a miracle, we should, upon your eviction in December, repossess this house as of January first. A pity, that (cough, cough). Good night, Mr. Dickens. Mrs. Dickens."

Bane left with a page of Cromwell stuck to one shoe.

Fog had seeped into the city, obliterating all signposts and benchmarks of the familiar as Barthomew Bane disappeared in the mist. It was unseasonably warm for October, and the infernal fog felt more like steam as it meshed with vapors from home fires and factories, clouding the city in a sulfuric mist.

Into the nighttime darkness, fog, and unknown, Charles Dickens, too, disappeared . . .

CHAPTER FIVE

harles Dickens knew the streets of London better than did any other man. Some nights he might walk ten miles, covering ground north and south from the park to the river, or east and west from the Tower to Westminster, or from his present to his past, from his dreams to his nightmares.

His pace slackened with the fog

which hindered his vision. Deftly using his cane, he tapped his way to find the sinkholes, sewers, and curbs. He felt himself pulled as though by a magnet, his childhood the negative pole.

At age twelve Charley had worked at a blacking factory, a rotting warehouse down by the river where he had pasted labels to pots. He seldom saw his father, jailed at the Marshalsea for dishonored debts. During those months, Charley had come to know, nook by cranny, the streets between the factory and garret where he had lived alone as a boy.

The memories swirled about him as another fog. He had endured sturdily enough the days of labor before he was rescued and sent back to school. In fact, Charley had worked at the factory some months after his father's release. His parents had needed help in supporting his siblings. So Charley toiled in danger and the dark while a sister, Frances, won prizes at the Royal Music Academy.

It was the totality of his abandonment that had always haunted him, for staying at the factory and forsaking school had not been his father's idea but his mother's. Elizabeth Dickens, so like him in many ways, a storyteller, mimic, humorist, his life source. She, of all people, treated him as a donkey trudging along, earning wages, eking out an existence so that the others might advance. He never voiced his all-engulfing grief that his mother Elizabeth should mortify him.

Dickens halted in his tracks, struck without warning

by the searing, ice-pick pain of neuralgia. Whenever it flared up, a damaged facial nerve incapacitated Charley. With luck, it could pass in minutes. Other times, the recurring condition left him disabled for days.

While Charley waited for his hurt to abate, the malodor of decay assaulted his senses. More than the stench of rotting food and vermin, this warm, wet night carried the unmistakable smell of death. Corpses stacked high in their shallow graves seeded clouds of putrefaction. The gases released in their decomposition proved dangerous, if not fatal, to the passerby.

Charley pulled from his pocket a handkerchief of cambric and covered his nose. He had paused, without knowing it, near a familiar cemetery. Mercifully, the neuralgia disappeared and Dickens continued on past the graveyard.

The thickening fog reduced his brain to a primal range, one of smell and touch and sound — a boat whistle, a horse's snort. A woman sobbing. Curses, shouts. The wails of an infant. The grunts of a brawl. Then —

A single, shattering, blood-chilling scream. Hackles rose on Charley's neck. A gut-wrenching cry . . . a moan of the damned. Running footsteps . . . shouting . . . Charles shoved aside by a seaman sprinting past, his guernsey spattered with bright red blood. He and Charles for a fleeting moment stared into each other's startled eyes. Dickens noted the man's blackened skin cancers.

A block away, Roger Knight lay dying, blood gushing from his severed neck, his dagger by his side. Over his body bent Paige, shrieking unnaturally like an animal gone to ground with no hope of life or salvation.

Dickens inched in the direction of the unearthly lamentation, tapping his way with his cane. The origin of the wails tricked his ears, shifting back and forth in the fog, coming first from one direction and then another, echoing and bouncing off walls. In this confusion, Charles stumbled, not having seen one sinkhole ahead of him.

Paige, hearing footsteps, picked up the dagger. From the fog, a sharp object jabbed at her. She leapt up, features twisted in rage. As though answering a challenge to a duel, the younger Knight hurled her cap to the ground, and from Paige's crown spilled a jet of black hair.

Paige Knight, age fourteen, now a girl alone on London's killing streets, defended the corpse of her adored only brother.

Ben Newborn emerged from the fog. He had jabbed Paige's shoulder with his crutch. Beholding the sorrowful scene, Ben could not at first believe that Roger lay lifeless at his sister's feet. Never would he have the chance to repay this young man who had helped him so much upon his arrival in London.

Handing his crutch to Paige, Ben picked up Roger's warm, limp body and slung it over his shoulder. Paige then used the crutch to feel their way through the fog. This funeral cortege slowly wended its way back to

Whitechapel. Soon Roger would join the others in the cemetery.

The fog lifted slightly so that Dickens regained his bearings. The river flowed only a block away. Slowly he edged toward Blackfriars Bridge, a signpost to his childhood of going home. It might as well have spanned the Styx, river of afterlives with no return.

From the bridge itself, Dickens stared into the Thames. He had come to the end of his way of life. He must forsake his writing and turn to the bar—if it would even admit him. He must dredge up the money for the immediate expenses. This he might do by selling more belongings. Perhaps he could solve such problems; but unlike the fog, his depression didn't lift.

Dickens watched a tiny eddy form in the water. How much easier it was to flow with the tide, not to push oneself but give up, give in, float downstream on the scudding surface of life.

He felt dead, very dead. Without feeling, anticipation, higher purpose, or hope.

Staring into the gurgling whirlpool, he lost all sense of the passage of time. He tried to see himself in the water but could not; the bridge was too high, the river too murky. For a second he imagined he saw the ghost of himself. That haggard face reflected his parents—grasping, selfish, squeezing out life. They were so lacking in light, John and Elizabeth, so hard and sharp, without love or fire.

These faces faded into another Charley, his own little

boy just five and a half years old. In this visage Dickens perceived neither himself nor his parents. He saw instead someone complete, whole, new. He heard a voice, "Papa, can you bring back a real Christmas?" and conjured the sight of an unborn baby, opaline eyelids shut tight, skin pink as peonies. Without doubt, Charley knew that this expected child was his own and a boy. He even knew its name.

Enraptured, Dickens stared. Past, present, and future. Melded in the soul, the promise of childhood.

That instant, the bass-toned bell of St. Paul's tolled the first of a dozen deep bongs. Midnight . . . the hour that belonged neither to today nor to tomorrow but only to the evanescent present. The rich, full, resonant voice of the bell banned from Charley's bones his fear of the past. The future approached and he was no longer afraid. Not *this* father. No John Dickens, no Josiah Squib, no Bartholomew Bane, would ever again threaten or taunt him. Never again would his spirit languish in the cells of fear or disgrace. He would fight—and he had the right weapons.

From within, his own carillon had rung, answering the apostolic knell of the bell and pealing the morning of his resurrection.

The room was dark, dark as the inside of a crypt on a moonless Hallowed Eve.

A soft thud . . . then the creaking of bolts bemoaning their hinges. Muffled footsteps—one, two. Again, silence.

A gas lamp flickered, blossomed into light. Then another. Shapes, though faint, grew visible in the dark. Bookcases. Side tables. A huge oaken desk.

About the room roved Dickens. Finding his match-box, he struck a phosphorus-dipped tip against hard flint. A flame shot up, blue at its base, gold at its crest.

The room lightened. Silent as a sorcerer recollecting a spell, Dickens sat at his desk, enkindled two candles. The flames undulated from the draft of the garden door, casting on the wall inspirited shadows that leapt about like spatting cats.

His incandescent eyes gleaming from inner sight, Dickens picked up his pen.

Fearless, fabulous, he attacked the blank page as his mind-fires found torchlight in the form of words: "Marley was dead: to begin with. There is no doubt whatever . . . "

From a source undiscernible to the human eye, the study gained in light until it glowed.

The next day, no one quite knew what had happened to Charles. He had burst through the door at 1:00 A.M., mulling again and again their street name. Despite the spelling, Marylebone was prounounced "Mar-lee-bun," and he had muttered several times "Mar-lee bones" as though trying to jog his memory. Charley loved to read through church registers for characters' names and had found at St. Andrew's, Holborn, a gold mine. He would borrow the name Marley from that church at the heart of the law courts. He liked the irony. Besides, it rhymed with Charley.

Dickens did not leave his study all day but wrote furiously while his children eavesdropped at the door. Their father paced and rehearsed his words until they flowed to perfection: "Oh! But he was a tight-fisted hand at the grindstone, Scrooge! A squeezing, wrenching, grasping, clutching, covetous, old sinner! Hard and sharp as flint, from which no steel had ever struck out generous fire; secret, and self-contained, and solitary as an oyster . . ."

So it went that day, Dickens inexplicably exuding energy as Catherine had never seen him do. This made not the slightest bit of sense. Only the night before, Charles had suffered from bleakness and anxiety. Now he was cheerful, even gleeful. Without flagging or fatiguing, he wrote into the night . . .

While after dinner, Boodle tried his own hand at magic. For nearly six years, the butler had watched his master conjure with his top hat, and in all this time, the butler had never figured it out. Neither had anybody else, but that made no difference to Boodle. As part of the act, he believed he should solve the mystery of the top-hat trick.

Disaster struck. The hat caught fire and Boodle panicked. He attacked it with a soda siphon, then threw the entire works into the trash. Upon beholding the damage done, Boodle gasped. He could never pay for a replacement.

Although it was midnight, the clock bonged two. Charles had slowed a bit, rested for a moment with head in hands. To help him fight sleep, he had left the garden door ajar. Startled by an eerie cry, he chided himself when he saw the raven. The black bird clung to a bare branch and spied, wings folded, head cocked.

Dickens had not seen in the garden a figure dressed all in black—black cloak, high hat, and clothing. He, like the raven, stared at Charley before floating through the door.

Before catching sight of him, Charley sensed him. He turned round and beheld in his study the Lord Protector Oliver Cromwell.

Rigid with amazement, the writer rose. Here stood the murderous Puritan who had seized power upon the execution of his king. Cromwell had restored Britain to greatness, but in a bloodbath from which the country had reeled. He had also stolen something infinitely precious, the Elizabethan soul of the land. Gone was Tudor delectation in life, the spirit of adventure, romantic love. Instead, a spiritual fog crept across Britannia—pessimism about man's better nature and his subjection to an angry God.

This tyrant Charles Dickens confronted. "What do you want with me, Lord Protector?" The evenness in his own tone surprised him.

The doleful visage looked right through him. "I killed Christmas and you know it. Pagan, popish twaddle! Sacrilege—all of it! Twelve days of knavery, and magic, and, and, and all that eating! Gluttony! Piggery! Jiggery-pokery! Stop what you are doing!"

"Why should I?" dared Dickens. Charley stood eye to eye with Cromwell, who shared with him some physical traits. Both were blessed with bountiful dark hair, Cromwell's just a bit lighter with its hazelnut tone. The skin of both men defied any type. Dickens sported a darkling look about him, his complexion tinted with a dollop of olive. Cromwell's face, however, looked bloodily ruddy as though he were rusting from the inside out. There, any commonalities ended.

In contrast to the handsome Dickens, Cromwell's big, bony nose dwarfed his thin lips, below which sprouted a farthing-sized wart. More warts mushroomed in his left eye socket. The heavily lidded eyes looked neither green nor gray but an undescribable hue of cinders or rain clouds flecked with holly greens. All such details the acutely observant Dickens noted.

The Lord Protector thundered, "As I banished Christmas, you would resurrect it. I will not brook such heresy in this land."

Dickens found his platform. "I must wonder what

power you might possibly have over me when you've been dead for, oh, about two hundred years."

Cromwell glided about the room, his lip curled upward in a sneer at the finery. "I am very much abroad in the afterlife."

Charles dared, "So is the Devil. Are you his advocate?"

"Fie!" Cromwell boomed across the ages. "You dare me, Charles Dickens, yet you cannot win. You were once before poor and so you shall be again. It matters not at all how you try to escape that. It is your fate. This wishfulness of yours for love and delight is pathetic . . . and you will pay for it." At this Cromwell raised a rough-knuckled finger at Dickens. "Hear me, for you do not know what my power is."

"I quite disagree, your lordship. I know what power lies in the human heart. That, I can reach as you cannot."

Cromwell hissed and drew back. "You snivelling scrivener to thwart me like this."

Dickens dismissed him with a wave of his hand, "Rot! I am a free man. I write my own story. Go somewhere else and play the ghost of Christmas past—that is, if anybody remembers you."

At that, Cromwell bellowed, pounced upon the manuscript sitting on Charley's desk. Dickens stepped sideways, blocked him. Cromwell raged, "These are not freely written, Charles Dickens. They will cost you everything that you hold dear. I bind you to your doom should you continue!"

They glared at each other, eye to eye, across the ages. Before Charley could respond, the hall clock struck.

A groggy Dickens pulled his head from his desk. He had fallen asleep and suffered a nightmare. Or had he . . . He leapt up and looked wildly about. All was safe, the study empty. For good measure, Charley checked behind the heavy curtains. No one hid there. He looked out onto the garden.

From his branch, the raven cawed. Dickens quickly shut the door to the parterre. Shaking his head to clear it, he headed straight for the pantry.

Dickens rummaged about the darkened storeroom until he found what he sought—a bottle of port. He uncorked it and poured himself a half glass. On second thought, he filled the stemware to the brim. Raising the glass in an unspoken toast to himself, he was struck by a sight too bizarre to fathom.

From an ash can protruded a burnt top hat.

Dickens downed his glass in a gulp.

It was time, Carlyle had decided. He only hoped that he hadn't waited too long.

Carlyle waited in the drawing room of One Devonshire Terrace, patting down the rain spots on his suit. He waited for Catherine, who was fitting the children. The two older ones needed clothes, which Catherine had decided to make. For anyone who knew Catherine, this development signaled alarm. Catherine couldn't sew.

Boodle wafted by, carrying a tray laden with a tea service. Carlyle jumped to his feet. The drop-leaf tea table hadn't been set up. The two leaves still hung straight down, and the legs hadn't been swung under to support the leaves. As Boodle swayed to and fro, Carlyle acted to avert disaster.

Entering with a gay "Hullo!" Catherine gave her guest her warmest welcome. To kiss the tall Scot on the cheek, she stood on tiptoe. Thomas was taken aback. Given her financial dilemma and advanced state of child-bearing, Catherine looked quite lovely.

"Sit!" she commanded. He did so obediently while Boodle escaped from the room. Catherine poured tea for Thomas but poured for herself only a cupful of milk. "It's so good to see you, Thomas. The last weeks of confinement grow tedious indeed."

"Ah! Yes! Quite!" Thomas felt addled and didn't know why. After making polite inquiries, he came to the purpose of his call. He asked with all the delicacy he could muster after their financial state. Her reply was not at all what he expected.

"Oh, but there's no reason to be concerned, Thomas! Charles will this afternoon explain to his publishers a new and secret project. He knows it will solve our problems, which are, of course, temporary." She sipped her milk in such an aura of calm, it actually made Carlyle nervous.

He wondered then if he inhabited the same planet as Charles and Catherine. Neither Dickens seemed to understand the horrors about to befall them should they not grasp instantly the gravity of their fix. "Catherine," he prodded, "have you considered letting go of your domestics?"

She cheerfully shook her head, no. "Out of the question! Boodle and Mrs. Plimpton have no other family." Noticing the depth of her dear friend's concern, she begged, "Please, please, don't worry about us!"

Catherine Hogarth Dickens lacked the capacity to in any way undermine her husband. This was born not of some girlish devotion but of rare insight into her husband's gifts. She took him seriously as a man of letters and had the specialized background to back up her judgment. She would never give away his failures, fears, anxieties, or doubts because she felt honor-bound to keep his trust. A loyal Gael, she remained true to her character at all times.

Thomas tried another approach. "What if Charles were to take up another calling? Turn his hand to journalism . . . or the law, perhaps." This was Carlyle's real hope. Charles had long deluded himself that writing fiction would earn him a living. It wouldn't. Even more, it would not earn him respectability as persons of real refinement and education could not even stomach his teary, treacly stories—no matter what Catherine thought.

Nonplussed, Catherine offered, "Feel free to speak to him, but it will do you no good. He must act on the life within him. That, I can understand." When Carlyle sighed, she reached over and patted his hand. "Do not worry if we lose this house. Charles is my real home."

Carlyle surrendered to the purity of her devotion. "Well, if your children go hungry, please don't feed them any more of my manuscripts!"

While across the hall, Dickens continued his attack on the executioner of Christmas: "They went, the Ghost and Scrooge, across the hall, to a door at the back of the house. It opened before them, and disclosed a long, bare, melancholy room, made barer still by lines of plain deal forms and desks. At one of these a lonely boy was reading near a feeble fire; and Scrooge sat down upon a form, and wept to see his poor forgotten self as he had used to be . . . "

Charley's mind drifted back to his own boyhood, which he could so plainly see.

That drizzly day, Paige Knight and the gang waited by a pit. Inside a group grave lay piles of sheeted bundles, a harvest of corpses ready for burial. Some had no shrouding but lay with their shut eyes facing the sky.

Roger Knight had been a sturdy youth; it took two laborers to carry his body. His limbs flopped about under his grimy bunting as the gravediggers carried him to the paupers' plot. They dumped his corpse right in front of the gang so that they might pray over Roger before consigning him to the hereafter. They were as silent as sheep bereft of their shepherd.

The youths bent their heads and murmured as though in prayer, though none had ever seen a Bible or the inside of a church except to raid the poor box or pick a vicar's pockets. This caused a delay in the doleful proceedings as Paige wracked her brain for something fitting to say.

Without a word or a crutch, Ben Newborn appeared. In his right arm he cradled a sheet of folded muslin. It was immaculately white and basted by Alice with a single lily and forget-me-nots along with the words: ROGER KNIGHT b. 1826 d. 1843.

A grateful Paige helped Ben rewrap Roger's body. Tears of grief and fatigue streaked her face as she, for the last time, cradled her brother. Ben could only say, "My sister was ten."

Drizzle turned to steady rain as they finished their task, yet none of the gang members left. Ben had brought with him another item, a folio. Seizing the moment, he began to read, Paige holding over him a jacket to shield the pages from the rain.

The sad, shabby little group seemed rooted to the soil as it heard for the first time the afflictions of Job. The power of the poetry, the richness of the faith, the trials of a righteous man, these Ben gave the gang. He read beautifully for the suffering his own soul had known and for his wish to honor God through words.

Others visiting Cheapside Cemetery wondered at the sight. There stood a dozen urchins braving the driving rain, not fleeing the awful spot but listening as though mesmerized to the rhapsodic lad in their midst.

Even the gravediggers listened, their flinty hearts softened, opened by Ben's reading.

CHAPTER SIX

n their offices on the Strand, Josiah Squib and Rufus Ledrook listened to the grand finale of Charley's presentation. Their expressions gave not a clue to their skepticism—if not sheer incredulity—at the proposal Dickens had made.

"With this fable of a miser's regeneration, we may be giving the people of our kingdom the fresh bread of hope, the fine wine of love, fit legacy from our nation's men of letters — so help me God, so rest my case." Dickens felt a tic in his cheek. He waited. Silence. "Well, gentlemen?"

While a confounded Squib looked to his partner, a wild-eyed Charley ran his hand again and again through his unkempt hair.

Finally Squib offered, "Cracked at last. And we saw it coming."

"I think the Hospital of St. Mary of Bethlehem might take him," offered Rufus. "They've moved to Lambeth, I hear."

Squib nodded. "Bedlam right across the river, Charley. You'll be close to family and friends."

Dickens flared, "Stop it! It's a positively ripping idea, and no one loses should we proceed apace with it."

Ledrook's hooded eyes zeroed in on him. "You would finish writing the whole story in just six weeks, by early December, yet you want it published by December seventeenth. That means the whole job — from script to bound books — must be done in barely two months."

"That's the idea!" Charley beamed.

Josiah continued, "Yours is a supernatural tale about Christmas, which is only celebrated anymore by bumpkins who can't read, much less purchase books, and who spend perhaps an hour or two commemorating the day."

"Now you've got it!" Dickens's eyes glistened with anticipation.

Ledrook lent his partner support. "By your reckoning, we will sell this book that people either can't read or can't buy and we will do so on a schedule that is virtually impossible to keep."

Dickens nodded vigorously.

Rufus Ledrook headed for the door, his words trailing behind him. "He's all yours, Josiah."

In a fever, Dickens got down to details. "I plan a first run of six thousand copies with steel engravings and woodcuts, fine leather bindings with gold trim —"

Josiah held up his hand. "Charles, enough!"

Dickens feigned a memory lapse. He had saved for last the linchpin of his pitch. "Did I forget? I shall pay all the printing costs!"

That did it. Losing all patience, Josiah snorted, "Charles Dickens, this is I, Josiah Squib. You forget. I know you have no money."

"But I will. That's the beauty of it." First wiping a stool with his handkerchief, he then sat. "If I pay for publication, I own the profits. I shall pay off your manufacturing costs with the profits from sales."

Josiah seemed to mull this. "Hmmm, that has been done. Still, why should I extend myself on a ghost story, one about a dead holiday whose daft author gives me migraines?"

"Because John Leech will illustrate it!" said Dickens, drawing on his gift for improvisational theater.

Taken off guard, Josiah scratched his scalp. "Well, I

must say, that does put a difference complexion on things. Leech sells fabulously well. How, did you secure his commitment?"

Dickens tried hard to sound offhand. "Does it matter?"

Dickens knew very well Josiah's partiality to artists. He had succeeded professionally on the shoulders of cartoonists like Robert Seymour, who had, rather disagreeably, killed himself. Other artists commanded equivalent sales and notices, but none more than the hotly sought Leech.

"Well, no," Josiah replied. "Still, the Chuzzlewit business cost us a pretty pence. We also agreed that you would go away should that story fail, which it promptly did, yet here you are."

Dickens, savoring the moment, stared right through Josiah. "You're seriously mulling this new proposal. I can always tell when you're seriously mulling as opposed to merely musing."

"Oh, shush!" Josiah spit back.

Sensing victory, Dickens added, "Did I tell you I want full-color woodcuts?"

John Leech knew nothing of the debate in which his name was so liberally being used. He and Dickens hardly knew each other. He sat at his drafting table, pen in hand, inking fine detail to a batch of new drawings. His fair, oily hair stood on end as he squinted, and grunted, and doodled.

A loud bang on the door jarred his hand. This did not sit well with a man whose shot nerves relished quiet. He ignored the knocker. Again—BANG! His lips compressed. BANG! BANG!

That did it. He rose—all six feet four inches of his frame. He stomped to the door like a fairy-tale giant, full of carnivorous ideas and a titanic body to back them up.

He literally flung open his door and saw on the top step Charley Dickens. He did not even recognize the author. "You the bloke's been banging on me door?"

"I am Charles Dickens." Hoping for a miracle, a concerned Charley pressed on, "You do know my name, don't you?"

Leech rubbed his chin, smearing it with ink. "You wrote that <u>Martin Swizzlestick</u>?"

Dickens held his tongue. With consummate control, he corrected the artist. "<u>Chuzzlewit</u>. And <u>Pickwick Papers</u> and <u>Oliver Twist</u>, too."

Leech brightened. "I know Twist. Pathetic little snot, he was, but that Fagin fellow, a right clever chap. Didn't someone get killed? A murder, it was! Oh, yes, I liked that."

Dickens forced a smile. "I'm so happy for you. I am publishing a new book which Ledrook and Squib has guaranteed. No need to serialize this tale, it's such a winner."

Leech looked impressed. "They guaranteed the whole thing?"

Dickens nodded. "Yes indeed, only I told them that I wouldn't dream of using a talent others than yours, so I came straightaway to you with an extraordinary offer inclusive of terms no other book illustrator has ever enjoyed." Dickens exhaled. He had so much at stake and it was growing cold and bleak as the heath. "Mr. Leech, may I come in?"

Leech stepped back. "Of course you may, little fellow. Call me John."

Dickens was not really short, but standing next to Leech, he looked like Jack in search of a beanstalk, standing next to John the Giant. He spent the next hour persuading the artist to participate in a deal that he had already told Squib was done. Charles was not by nature a prevaricator but could, in a pinch, use his God-given gift for fiction to color the facts. He did this in service to a cause he thought just—at least most of the time.

Once the minds of artist and writer had met, Dickens rushed to tell Carlyle the good news. Thomas, wrapped in a metaphysical fog, waited at his club. He had a keen sense of the divine which illuminated his histories with the light of eternity. Thus, once Charles arrived and joined him, Thomas heard little of what his friend had to say. He punctuated his conversation with "Uh-huh," "Splendid," "Do tell!" until the import and thrust of Charley's news finally penetrated his skull. Once it had, he erupted. "What!" the Scot exclaimed. "Just how many copies must you sell before realizing a profit on this harebrained scheme?"

Charles hesitated. "Well, I've priced it a bit low so that the poor may have it, which means I'll have to sell the entire run." He paused again before delivering the coup de grâce. "That is to say, we need to sell all six thousand copies quickly."

A disbelieving Carlyle responded in funereal tones, "In other words, you're giving it away. You're pricing low for the poor a gold-trimmed, leather-bound book with full-color engravings. Charles, how can you?"

Growing defensive, Charley parried, "It's the right thing! I know that it is. Only by paying for the book's publication can I own it free and clear and keep the lion's share of the profits, not some paltry sum like royalties. Thomas, I need money now. My family contines to grow."

Carlyle leaned back in his chair, motioned away the retainer attempting to serve their turtle soup. "Oh, Charles," he lamented. "I had no idea that you would agree to such a ruinous deal with your publishers. I'm scandalized that they even accepted your terms."

"Leech is part of it, don't forget." Charles felt stung

that Thomas didn't applaud his plan but received it with pessimism, even doom and disdain.

Carlyle's overgrown eyebrows twitched. "That won't guarantee success. And if you fail, might your family not see the inside of a poorhouse? Have you any idea what that's like?"

Tensions rising, Charley let the question hang. "Really, Thomas, do you think I would take that kind of risk with my children?"

Thomas leaned forward. "That is exactly the risk you are taking! You can't know if the bar will admit you or a newspaper take you back should your enterprise end in failure."

"It won't!" Charley dug in.

"How can you be so sure?"

"I can't explain it." Charley's defenses had swung shut, barring further criticism or challenges.

Grown too frantic to keep silent, Carlyle rued, "How could Catherine have given her consent to this?"

Charley warned, "Not a word of this to her! The child is due in another ninety days and this venture might imperil her health, cause her needless worry."

Had Carlyle not already succumbed to shock, these words might have vexed him greatly. He did, however, grasp the ghastliness of the idea that Catherine knew nothing of her husband's addlepated plan. Charley sought to reassure him. "Thomas, my accounts won't be payable until January of next year. By that time, the book will have succeeded, I'll have paid off its debts, and spared Catherine all that worry. All I need is ninety days, same as the child."

Carlyle motioned the server. "Your life, Charles, is a Hall of Doom. Garçon, two cognacs. Make that Martel, Cordon D'or."

Dickens shook his head. "No, thank you."

Carlyle snapped, "They're for me!"

While Carlyle contemplated the worst of fates for his friend, Ben Newborn confronted a single, ugly reality.

Alice McManus, her pallor cadaverous, drifted in and out of sleep. By her side, Ben sat and read aloud from a small and well-thumbed volume. A flickering lantern made shadow play on the wall of Ben's well-cast features.

"Ah! County Guy, the hour is nigh
The sun has left the lea,
The orange-flower perfumes the bower,
The breeze is on the sea.
The lark, his lay who trill'd all day,
Sits hush'd his partner nigh;
Breeze, bird, and flower confess the hour,
But where is County Guy?"

Ben paused and saw that Alice smiled. He continued to read:

"The village maid steals through the shade
Her shepherd's suit to hear;
To Beauty shy, by lattice high,
Sings high-born Cavalier.
The star of Love, all stars above,
Now reigns o'er earth and sky,
And high and low the influence know —
But where is County Guy?"

" 'Twas lovely, laddie," said Alice weakly.

" 'Twas the great Sir Walter Scott," said Ben.

She gave gim a roguish grin. "Sounded like an Irishman to me!" Ben laughed. She reached out and grabbed his hand. "You know I loves you as though you were me own. I knows you know that. Just don't ever lose your power to do good, boyo. If you do, you'll be powerless."

Ben looked at her blankly. She pressed, "A bad person can't do good even if he wanted to. Not for the right reasons, anyway. You can choose. Good or evil. That all by itself gives you power."

This effort had taken her strength. Eyes closing, she drifted off in a reverie. "On the far side, I'll say hullo to yer ma and pa and li'l sister. I promise you."

Ben protested vigorously. "You're not dying, Alice."

"Only to this world, laddie, only to this world."

A frustrated Ben watched Alice fall into sleep, the painkiller of the poor. He slept fitfully that night, as did . . .

Charley Dickens. Restless and resentful, Dickens fell into a fitful slumber.

Phantoms peopled his dreamworld. There, that lad from Parliament, the one with the crutch. He materialized from a mist. Charley handed him a little book, which the boy seemed jubilant to see.

Then who should appear but the Lord Protector, Oliver Cromwell. He snatched the precious text and shredded the pages with his talonlike hands. With a diabolical grin on his face, he threw the leaves to the wind. Enraged, Charley assailed Cromwell and was shocked to see that the Puritan wore the face of —

Carlyle.

Dickens awoke with a jolt.

His dream horrified him. As frustrated as he felt with the Scot, whose respect and approval he never quite earned, Carlyle was not his enemy. Cromwell was. Dickens made no sense of this muddle.

The baffling dream haunted him all morning as he dressed and headed for Ledrook and Squib.

Not finding Josiah and Rufus in their offices, Charley stepped out onto the lane where the printer's shack stood. From this direction, Charles heard voices — angry voices. He headed toward them, catching as he went snatches of a dispute: "Dammit, John, you've lost your senses!" That was Josiah, definitely. Another voice: "You'll lose more than your senses if you go through with this!" That sounded like John Leech.

Dickens arrived at the door to the shack and saw backed up against the wall the engravers and typesetters. In their midst, Josiah Squib and a furious John Leech stared each other down.

Incredulous, Dickens entered to see page proofs and galleys lying all about. "Whatever is the matter here?" he asked.

Leech turned and glowered at him. "Ah'll tell you what's the matter, dear! These colorers ain't fit to do the likes of me drawings. Look at what these apes been doin' for a living!"

Leech picked up a stack of page proofs and tore each in half, sending all, flying one by one, up to the ceiling.

Dickens and Squib lunged after the papers. "Stop this! Are you mad!" Charley hollered.

Squib let them all know, "I am not paying for these!"

Fuming, Leech stormed out, remonstrating all the way, "I thought you had real printers—not some color-blind buffoons! Look at the work they do! No self-respecting goat would eat it!"

Squib came to the point. "He's revoked his permission to publish his drawings. No Leech, no printing, no sales—no deal."

Dickens, nerves already frayed, had no time or

energy to spare. "It's your fault he's gone. You always skimp on materials. Cheapskate! Skinflint!"

Josiah's eyelids quivered. "Oh, if that doesn't do it! You give me no time, no budget, no support. I'm done with you, you, you, Charles . . . Knuckleby, Twisted, Chuzzletwit . . . " He motioned at the door. "Out! Out! Out, out, out! Go on, out of here!"

Dickens, pupils shrunk to nothingness, turned on him. "Next to you, Scrooge is Lady Bountiful."

With flapping arms, Josiah raged, "Oh, that does it, that really does it! A pox on your house, a plague on your privy, may all your remaining manuscripts never see the light of day nor the dark of printer's ink! Out, out!"

Squib virtually ejected Dickens and locked the door behind him. The workers in the shack cowered before their rabid employer.

Dickens looked toward the darkening sky. The bells of St. Mary-le-Strand bonged the hour, grew louder and louder until Charley covered his ears.

Church bells tolled, too, in Whitechapel, where an impassioned Ben Newborn pleaded with the apothecary. Time after time, the store owner shook his head, no. Ben persisted, his balled fist resting on the counter. Without further ado, the apothecary showed Newborn the door.

Once he was on the street, tears of frustration threatened Ben's composure. He looked up and saw Paige Knight's sorrowful face. The two, for a moment, locked gazes.

. . . Just as a dazed Charles Dickens trudged up Marylebone Road. He stood long and looked hard at his home on the Terrace. Many minutes passed before he could square his shoulders and enter his house.

Poised for a raucous welcome, Charles was surprised to see an empty hallway. The clock ticked too loudly. He called out for his children. None came. Worried, he called for his housekeeper, who not long thereafter descended the stairs. "Mrs. Plimpton," Charles asked, "where is everyone?"

From the expression on Minnie's face, Dickens knew that something serious was amiss. She chose her words with care. "The children are in their rooms. Your physician is with Mrs. Dickens. She nearly lost the child today. He says she could lose it still. I am sorry, sir."

Dickens dashed to the steps, but Mrs. Plimpton gently impeded him. "She is exhausted and requires rest. It's the children. They are so frightened. They're the ones who need you now."

He nodded, his throat constricted so tightly that he could hardly swallow. This day, he had lost a book and very nearly a baby. Carlyle was right. The time had come to give up the ghosts.

Then he remembered the vision of his unborn, the fragile little traveler suspended between Earth and the other world. Bringing this infant home, safe and whole, was all that mattered to Charles Dickens.

CHAPTER SEVEN

ost in thought, Josiah Squib teased himself with a goose-feather pen, dragging its quill back and forth across his chin. He alternately squinted and arched his eyebrows, swinging from deep meditation to outright amazement.

<u>A Christmas Carol</u>, pages neatly stacked, lay upon his desk. As Josiah grazed through the pages,

Rufus craned his head through the door. "You wanted to see me?" his partner asked.

Josiah dropped the pen and leaned back in his chair, hands pressed together in a prayerful pose. He said very quietly, "It's gold, Rufus. Dickens has written pure, unalloyed, twenty-four Karat gold. No wonder he wants to own it."

"Humph." Rufus, disgruntled, entered Josiah's office. "I can't see how that's good news. If he owns it, that's your doing."

Squib shook his head back and forth. "No, do not underestimate me, Rufus Ledrook. What if he couldn't pay his manufacturing costs?"

Rufus sat, his wide-spreading waistline barely contained by the chair. "If the book is that good, of course he'll profit and pay off his costs."

Squib cast a deliciously devilish look at his partner. "Maybe not. Suppose he ran into some . . . unforeseeable expenditures."

Rufus, looking askance at his partner, asked, "Such as?"

"Well, well, well." Squib toyed with his associate. "What if it cost too much to recolor Leech's drawings? Or what if he couldn't sell enough copies? After all, he's printing six thousand, and that's quite a few for a dead author in England."

Rufus, too, leaned back. He understood the tack Josiah was taking, but wouldn't tip his hand as yet. So he pretended, "You've lost me, Josiah. If he couldn't pay, we would be left with the losses. How could that possibly be good news?"

Josiah, triumphant, stood. "Because his inventory would be ours! We take possession of the unsold stock and own this blasted masterpiece!"

Rufus looked like a goldfish as his lips repeatedly formed the letter 'O.' "Well, well, yes, we might, but how can you be so confident in your opinion of this work?"

Squib scoffed, "It's my business to guess such things. That's why I'm your partner. Believe me, this work will outsell anything Dickens ever did."

Rufus shook his head. "I don't know, Josiah . . . "

"Come, come, Rufus! He's forever abusing us with his harangues and accusations. Only last year, he virtually charged us with stealing from him. Who all along footed the bills when his work failed to sell?"

"We did!"

"Who took the risk of hiring him to write <u>Pickwick Papers</u> in the first place!"

"We did!"

"What about that bloodsucking father of his, begging us for loans?"

"Ha! We never even let on to Charles about that!"

Squib sounded like a colonel rousing his hussars to battle. "Why should we tolerate any more abuse from this man? Why not just give him what he has all along believed? By the cross of St. George, let's steal from him!"

Rufus shot to his feet. "Ssshh! Heavens! Take care! You never know who might overhear."

Strangely, this turn of events energized Josiah as though, from a secret sort of vengeance, he had gained strength with each word he uttered. Having rationalized a vindictive premise, Josiah could now plummet head-long into the sort of argument that can justify any injustice one chooses.

"Oh, wouldn't it be perfect! I tell you," he said, pacing behind his desk. "Poetic justice, this. I've taken so much guff from that man over the years. Let his suspicions prove self-fulfilling prophecy because if he accuses us of skulduggery, nobody will believe him! He's *always* feeling persecuted."

At that, Rufus guffawed. "I should say so. The man is forever on a tear. And his threats to the social order! Advocating universal education and all that nonsense. Humbug. To stop him, we'd be doing the country a favor!"

Josiah slammed a balled fist into the palm of his free hand. "That's it! It's a patriotic task we undertake." Silence. "Does that make us undertakers?"

The two men groaned at the pun, which seemed, however, eerily appropriate. Yes indeed, as undertakers, they discussed in detail their plan for burying Charley Dickens.

Unaware of any plot, Dickens sat alone in his garden

facing one short and lopsided little fir. The tree seemed to stare back at him . . .

Just as Ben Newborn, huddling to keep warm, crouched by London Bridge and stared cross-river. He could see the towers of Southwark Cathedral, a vision of stolidity and calm in the manufacturing maelstrom that southern London had become. Ben didn't feel a thing as he looked blankly at these surroundings. He didn't even feel the chill wind that bit his hands and nipped his face.

Then . . . THUNK! From over one shoulder, a brown paper bag dropped into his lap. Startled, Ben jumped to his feet, nearly fumbling the parcel. He craned his neck to see Paige Knight leaning against a bridge pier.

Paige nodded at him. *Open the bag*, her eyes said. This, Ben did. Upon seeing the sack's contents, Ben dropped to his knees and howled like a wolf pup saved from a storm.

The bag contained a bottle of medicine for Alice.

On Catherine Dickens's nightstand stood her empty medicine bottle. By the bedside sat her husband, looking lost and younger than his years. Again and again he had apologized to her, and again and again she has said— don't blame yourself. He promised he would secure regular employment, but she cut him off. "What about your new story?" she asked.

Dickens shrugged his shoulders. "You read it, and if you like it, I shall be content."

"Where is the manuscript?" she asked. Catherine looked alarmingly pale, her creamy complexion discolored a chalky white.

He gathered his courage. "Catherine, don't worry about it. Understand me, the project is scuttled. Dismiss it from your mind. You have more important matters to consider now."

She gave him a wary look. "You lost your temper, didn't you?"

He wouldn't answer for many seconds. "I tried not to, Catherine, really I tried."

She smiled in spite of herself and stroked his hair. "This book has caused you such anxiety. Put your mind at ease. We'll manage. We always have." Pain shot through Catherine's sweet features as a spasm attacked, constricted her body.

Too anxious to talk until the danger passed, Charley clasped Catherine's hand, transfusing her with his strength. For three minutes he held on to his wife. The spasm abated.

Catherine's eyes widened, giving her the look of a child suddenly presented with a long-hoped-for pony. "Charles, you've named this book for yourself."

Caught off-guard by her remark, he ran reflexively a hand through his hair. "Whatever made you think of that at a time like this!"

"It helps to keep my mind off the baby. When I worry, it only grows worse." Catherine's eyes had turned pleading.

Charley saw instantly the value in distracting her. Doing his best to sound buoyant, he replied, "No, I didn't realize it. I thought of a carol as a hymn, a song for Christmas. Now that you mention it, Carol is the Latin for Charles, like King Charles . . . "

"Beheaded by the Puritans and succeeded by Cromwell!" Catherine beamed in satisfaction at having finished his thought. Savoring this moment of harmony, the two discovered together ironies in the title A <u>Christmas Carol</u>. Given this pleasure, Catherine's pain eased. Her unborn escaped one more peril.

Charley promised her that she should never again worry, not about herself, not about the baby. Within the week, he would find a steady job. Though to himself he doubted that he would ever pass the bar or that any newspaper in England would have him. They must know he was passé. In London, failure made one as welcome as a leper.

The next morning, sunlight cleft the clouds as would a golden-bladed saber, striking the dome of St. Paul's Cathedral and irradiating its cross with a heavenly light. Beneath strolled Benjamin, clothes clean, hair trimmed, shoes cobbled. He wielded his crutch as though it were a malacca cane. Dressed as he was, Newborn looked a different person, his purposeful stride carrying him at a quick clip down Fleet Street and up the Strand.

At No. 186, Josiah and Rufus checked a calendar. If Charley's book was not bound by December 17, the writer couldn't possibly have enough time to sell it by Christmas. That way they could take possession of an intact inventory as early as February of the next year.

As they double-checked the printing schedule against the calendar, a soft rap on the door escaped their notice. Quietly, persistently, the rap came again. As though warding off a bottle fly, Josiah flapped and called out, "Yes, what is it!!"

The door opened slowly, creakily. There in the doorframe, backlit by surprise sunlight, stood a very young man leaning on a crutch. Both Josiah and Rufus blinked. Said Rufus tentatively, "Your name wouldn't be Tim, would it?"

"Benjamin Newborn, sir, but I go by Ben. I apologize for this intrusion, but there was no one in your front room."

Josiah clicked his tongue in irritation. "Well, what is it? Can't you see we're in conference?"

Ben stepped forward and handed Squib a card—the calling card of Charles John Huffam Dickens, signed in ink for good measure.

Josiah gave him the sharp-eyed look of an eagle

scouting a grassland for lunch. "However did you get this, boy?" He handed the card to Rufus.

Unrattled, Ben explained, "Mr. Dickens gave it to me outside Parliament. We were discussing politics and educational reform."

"Uh-huh," interjected a skeptical Ledrook. "I say you picked his pocket, what about that, huh, huh?"

Ben looked at Rufus as though he were a bit thick. "Had I chosen to pick his pocket, he wouldn't own a gold watch right now. I mean, why would a ragamuffin like me steal a card, the theft of which could lead me nowhere but here where Mr. Dickens would disown me to you both?"

Josiah grunted. "Yes, well, get on with it. Why are you here?"

"To discuss with you my prospects for employment."

"Oh, that!" Josiah smacked his brow in mock amazement. "Forgive me for not guessing from the first! Just because a publisher's apprentice must be able to read and write perfectly is no reason for us to discount your prospects for employment."

Rufus smirked, "Have you even been to school, boy?"

"No, sir, I haven't."

The two men looked at each other and shrugged. Ben, unfazed, explained. "My mother taught me to read. We both worked in the iron mines of Birmingham. On

Sundays she sang at our church while the rector and his vicar advanced my studies. I am now sixteen years old. My English is flawless, my Latin fair, but my Greek only a beginner's."

Rufus exclaimed, "Oh, then it's settled! You can just bypass lower school and go straight on to Cambridge. What do you say, Josiah? He's got Latin and Greek."

"Oh, I don't know." Josiah drummed his fingers on his chin. "He looks more like the Oxford type to me."

Ben ground his back teeth. "I lost my family . . . an explosion, but I don't expect you to believe me. Our vicar back in Birmingham can confirm what I've told you."

"No doubt you read to each other the odes of Pindar." Instantly Josiah's mood shifted to darkness. "Listen, young man, I know this signature. This card is real. I recognize better than anyone in England the inimitable penmanship of Charles Dickens. Just why did he send you here?"

"In truth, he knows nothing of my being here. I came of my own accord."

Rufus leaned forward. "Then you're not here because of his new work?" Ben shook his head, no.

Rufus and Josiah huddled in a corner, taking less than two minutes to decide that Ben could prove useful—in more ways than one. Josiah picked up a stack of paperwork and handed this to Ben. "All right then, show us how clever you are. Read this aloud, flawlessly, of course, and catch as you go any spelling errors that might appear in this stave."

Ben's features constricted as he beheld the new work. He cleared his throat. He would give the reading of his life . . .

And he did. Josiah and Rufus hung on his every word until Ben began Stave V of the <u>Carol</u>:

> "I will try to honor Christmas in my heart and try to keep it all the year. I will live in the Past, the Present, and the Future. The Spirits of all Three shall strive within me. I will not shut out the lessons that they teach . . . Heaven and Christmas Time be praised for this!"

Silence. Ben looked to the publishers for a reaction. Josiah marveled at the boy's performance, read not only with absolute fluency but with the expression of one who had fully apprehended all nuances of the material. Aloud he only offered, "Outside, lad. My partner and I need to talk."

Drained of emotion, Ben departed without uttering a word. He had hardly shut the door behind him when Rufus beat Josiah to the punch. "We could use an extra pair of hands for Christmas, what with Charles tying up so many of our employees. Besides, you're always on the lookout for an able apprentice, aren't you?" Josiah gave Rufus, the hiring partner, an unblinking stare.

"Hmmm. I agree," Josiah offered, "He's journeyman material, I do not doubt, but we'll need to keep an eye on him every minute. We can't be sure he's trustworthy."

Josiah Squib walked into the hallway and extended a hand to Benjamin Newborn. "Welcome to Ledrook and Squib, young man."

Numbly, dumbly, Ben shook hands. He had fully expected that the publishers would hire him, yet when they actually did, he couldn't believe it. No, this couldn't be true. From a Whitechapel slum he had come to the Strand and secured employment with a publishing firm.

Wait until he told Alice McManus!

Later in the day, the printer's shack looked like a meeting of mercury-maddened hatters. Engravers dunked metal sheets in acid baths; carvers hastily chopped new woodblocks. Compositors rushed about with racks of movable type. Dyers prepared batches of gilt while others mixed the primary colors.

In the midst of this mayhem, Josiah Squib directed traffic. He must appear to exhort them ever onward, yet what he really wanted was a slowdown — if not stoppage. This caused him to send confusing signals such as, "Take your time . . . as much time as you like!" or "Print in haste, repent in leisure!" Even he knew he was not making sense.

Into this frenetic scene strode a bewildered Charles Dickens. "What on earth are you doing, Josiah?"

"What does it look like? Printing your story!" Josiah's arms flapped in fake excitement, making him look less airborne than palsied.

Dickens tried to speak, but his voice betrayed him. Confounded, he could only stammer, "But John Leech . . . I . . . We fought . . . Who knew? . . . Why?"

Josiah patted him on the back as though that would stop Charley's stammer. "Oh, we sorted out John, all right. He agreed to hand-tinted pictures and final approval of his illustrations. An extra expense, but a necessary one. No worries now!"

Dickens could still not adjust to this meteoric shift in his fate. Squib, looking craftily at the writer, then over to Ben, asked Dickens, "I don't suppose you see a familiar face?"

All faces were a collective blur to Dickens. He looked about the room and shook his head. Josiah offered, "Let me help you." He pointed to the table where Ben Newborn labored.

Ben looked up and saw to his joy Charles Dickens standing in the doorway. At the same instant, Dickens saw Newborn. The author stared in vague recognition, but his memory yielded no exact identification.

Josiah peeped over his bifocals. "Don't you know our newest apprentice? He's setting lead for us."

Charley's glance ensnared the crutch leaning against Ben's table. The image clicked. He raised a finger, pointing at the lad. "Master Newborn!" he bellowed for all the room to hear. "Prime Minister Peel wanted a word with you!"

Like an anchor into an ocean of noise, silence fell hard. Instant quiet . . . until a typesetter dumped on the floor his tray of metallic letters. Incredulous that the new boy might know the prime minister, all swung their eyes in Ben's direction.

Josiah uttered to himself, "Prime Minister Peel?"

Dickens and Ben shared a conspiratorial smile. Deciding to pursue this line to its limit, Dickens capped off with, "Thomas Carlyle did not appreciate your walking off like that. You never answered his question about Sir Walter Scott."

. . . Suppressed chortles, guffaws from the floor. The employees relished the unprecedented sight of Josiah Squib struck speechless.

At that instant, Charles smacked his forehead. "Law, no! Catherine! I promised her!" And he dashed out the door.

Josiah had trouble recovering his poise as he sidled up to Ben Newborn's table. He stared at the lad, who wouldn't look up from his work. Several seconds passed. Finally Squib demanded in a low voice, "The truth, boy. You did learn some Greek."

With eyes still on his task, Ben replied, "The grammatical structures are not unlike Latin's. Only the alphabet throws you off at first."

Josiah recoiled. Ancient Greek was a very difficult language to learn, and had Ben found it easy, he might prove too intelligent to control.

Charles Dickens, by contrast, lost all control as he rushed homeward, worrying all the way—what if Catherine hadn't liked the story? He had never before written of ghosts or Christmas or in the style of the <u>Carol</u>. What if she found the new work inferior? Found no faith in it? In him? Then what! How could he convince her to give him the time he needed to finish this job?

Fraught with fear, he flung open the door to Number One. He was arrested by the sight of Catherine standing at the top of the stairs, his manuscript in hand. Love, hope, anxiety—all enkindled her eyes as well as his. Alarmed at finding her up and about, Charles started to speak, but she shushed him with a gesture, placing a finger to her lips.

Her voice was soft. "I married magic!"

CHAPTER EIGHT

ith so little time until the deadline, employees worked furiously at Ledrook and Squib. Each morning Mr. Dickens arrived at the printer's shop and exhorted them all to hurry, hurry. In the afternoon Mr. Squib entered and urged them all not to exhaust themselves. Little pieces of equipment disappeared. Dye batches were

botched. Racks were mislaid for days. Astonishingly, Squib seemed not at all annoyed by these setbacks. Instead, he joked about elves spoiling the Christmas project while Ledrook chortled lamely at these feeble jests. Something odd was afoot, no doubt.

The first week, Josiah handed Charley the stack of invoices for labor to date. Dickens took these home and punctiliously recorded each in a ledger he kept for the project: "Two Steel Plates, 1 Pound; Printing Plates, 17 Pounds 6 Shillings," and so on.

At the same time, Ben kept the first of several secret meetings.

He hurried home up Ludgate Hill with its crown of St. Paul's Cathedral. Night had fallen, and with it any promise of safety. Ben turned south onto an unlit lane that wended its way between the cathedral and river. His eyes never rested but continually scanned the streets and corners for dangers.

"Pssst!" Ben heard. He tensed, pivoted to look behind him. Again, "Pssst!"

Ben relaxed. "Where are you?" he called in a wary voice.

"Over here!" Paige Knight, backlit by a torch, stepped forth into the alley.

Ben walked toward Paige and the light. Despite the chill and damp of the evening, flecks of sweat beaded Ben's forehead. "What's the matter?" Paige asked. "You're not sick, is you?"

Ben shook his head vigorously. "I'm well. Very well. Here." Ben pulled from inside his jacket a cardboard-bound folio and opened it. Paige looked inside, but the contents confused her. Within the folio lay featherweight pages of gold-colored matter. She shrugged. "What in the name of Guy Fawkes is this!"

"Gold leaf," Ben said. Paige clicked her tongue. Ben pressed on, his words hurried, "Once the book goes to binding, they'll use this on the covers and edges of the pages."

"Can I pick one up?" Ben nodded. Paige gently lifted a sheet, fingering for the first time this exotic substance from the printer's world. "Light as an angel feather!" The delicate gold leaf lay airily on Paige's palm.

"That's the advantage," Ben explained. "I can easily lift this, a few leaves a day. By the end of the printing run, I'll have enough for a physician who can cure Alice for good. You do with your cut what you will. You sure you know someone who can handle this?"

Paige frowned, sucked on her inner cheek. "Dunno. I'll have to find out its value out here. If it's mixed with another metal, well, who can tell what it's worth? A dolly shop or pawnbroker, maybe."

Ben panicked. "No, don't! A pawnbroker would think it was stolen."

Paige laughed. "This is London, Ben. He'd *know* it was stolen."

Unsure, Ben warned, "Be careful, will you. Ask someone you can trust."

Paige thought for a moment. "There's one, MacPherson. Wouldn't your Dickens use a pawnbroker he could trust?"

Ben guffawed. "I doubt he's spoken to a pawnbroker in his life. The man's rich, depend upon it."

Paige stared at Ben as though he were rock-headed. "Then why is he hocking stuff at MacPherson's?"

Ben started to speak but gave up. He had no idea what Paige meant. Surely the girl mistook her facts, but he decided not to say so. Like many girls, Paige argued a lot — or so thought Benjamin Newborn.

At One Devonshire, Dickens penned the final flourishes for his Christmas story. He was satisfied, deeply satisfied. With Ignorance and Want, he had scored the points he tried to convey to Commons. With Past, Present, and Future, he could show Britain the crossroads of her agrarian past and her future as an industrial power. We need not fear that future, he sensed, if only the miserly among us would open their hearts to the needy masses. Christmas served as the perfect occasion on which to preach this joy in *caritas* — love of one's fellow mortals manifest in benevolent acts. In shared strength, we might travel into that dark — our unknowable futures — with the way illuminated by the fires of love.

Unbeknownst to him, a conspiracy unfolded above him.

In the garret, Mrs. Plimpton, Mamie, and Charley tried to keep quiet as they cut and pasted colored papers in the shapes of bells, stars, and pine trees. None was particularly coordinated or artistic. Their creative results reduced them to giggles. Little Charley without mercy teased Mamie, who had covered herself with glue.

In the pantry, Boodle fought keen disappointment. Times had indeed grown tough. They had run out of port. A nip of that sauce usually eased his aches, but now they were out, completely out, of his only anesthetic. Boodle settled for a gin. He hated the stuff. From deep within his being, a sigh escaped.

In the morning, Dickens struck forth in great anticipation. Today promised another giant stride toward publication. Pimlico Paperworks would deliver the high-grade stock Dickens had special-ordered.

As Dickens hurried to work, two burly deliverymen unloaded their horse-drawn wagon. The teamsters strained as they carried inside the heavy, packaged reams and shelved them in the printer's shack. The others paused in their labors and gathered to watch as the chief printer and his aide, Philobuster and Bob, sampled the costly stock. Upon opening one package, Philobuster smiled as would a wine steward in uncorking Château Lafite.

Fingering the exquisite paper, he told his fellow, "He wanted the best and he got the best, all right."

Bob frowned. "I never before saw Mr. Squib order this quality of paper."

"Not Squib, Dickens!"

"What do you mean?"

Hearing the name Dickens, Ben stopped in his tracks and joined the others. He heard Philobuster expound, "You don't know? Charles Dickens is paying all the costs for his <u>Carol</u>."

Bob and the others murmured in wonderment. They'd never heard of such a thing before. Ben didn't believe it. "Why would Mr. Dickens pay?" he asked no one in particular. He could not mentally process the single, horrific thought that he had stolen gold leaf not from Squib but Dickens.

At that moment Squib scurried in and saw all of his workers transfixed as in tableau. "Very good! Take a break! No need to knock yourselves out!"

One of the teamsters handed Squib an invoice. "You're not Dickens, I know, but you'll do. Sign here! Fifty-nine quid, it is!" And sign, Squib did.

Josiah scanned the invoice, which read, "Pimlico Paperworks. Stock: 59 Pounds 5 Shillings."

Feeling uneasy, he looked up to see Benjamin staring right through him. Brandishing the invoice, Squib shooed away both Ben and the deliverymen. "Can't have Mr. Dickens worrying about these, now can we?"

Squib shot out the door, across the lane, and into the storefront facing the Strand. Straight to his office he strode, slamming the door behind him. Once finished with his little chore, he would have a nearly perfect mate to the bill he clutched. It would look the same, it would feel the same. There would be just one major difference. The cost of the paper would rise magically to eighty-nine pounds fifteen shillings. The resultant forgery would land in the lowest right-hand drawer of Josiah Squib's desk.

In that drawer he had already stacked a counterfeit batch of bills.

Josiah plopped into his chair, rubbed his hands. Not much longer. His calendar said December 14. Tomorrow the presses would run. On the sixteenth, the books would be bound. No, not much longer at all.

The book's birthday arrived. An assembly line of highly skilled and speedy workers would take <u>A Christmas Carol</u> from the press to bound books. The employees who had finished their own work observed the process, filled with pride in this finely wrought volume. Ben, who had never before seen any of these procedures, witnessed the undertaking with awe.

The printed signatures were sewn together while an apprentice glued endpapers to the hand-sewn signatures.

On the next table, a journeyman knocked the assembled book into a square, trimming as he went any rough edges exposed on the side. As his second step, he applied to the book's spine a coating of glue. Each volume was then placed in a vise and hammered until the spine turned convex. A headband was sewn to the top of the spine and anchored every few stitches to the kettle stitches below.

On the last table, a supervisor affixed to each and every copy a hand-tooled, hand-stamped, salmon-colored cloth cover. The cover was next pasted to both the book's spine and wooden boards. The edges were turned and smoothed around the boards; the outside endpapers were pasted to the boards' inside surfaces.

The binder walked over to Dickens and handed him the nearly finished product. The writer's name, encircled by holly leaves, had been stamped on both front and back covers.

It was quiet as a church nave at midnight as Dickens turned over and over in his hand a copy of the book. He opened it, turning to the blue and white title page that boldly declared <u>A Christmas Carol</u>, by Charles Dickens.

Dickens, muted by joy, did not say a word.

Neither could Ben Newborn think of anything to say to Mr. Dickens, whose kindness had led him to this magical moment. Greatly troubled, Ben watched Dickens depart with a handful of copies. He took Ben's heart with him, too. Never in his life would Ben have wittingly cheated Charles Dickens.

Having savored the fruits of their labors, the binders and stitchers went back to work. Only 5,996 more copies to go!

A grueling though happy day passed at the printer's. The workers enjoyed an exhilirating sense of exhaustion, the kind of cheery fatigue born of doing beautifully a Herculean task. Their mood was infectious. Laughter, whistling, and singing could be heard throughout the day and well into the evening.

As the last work shift came to an end, Tucker the binder handed Ben a folder. "Do me a favor, lad. Take these up to Mr. Squib. They're for the sums on the covers."

"Shouldn't they go to Mr. Dickens?" Ben argued.

"No, laddie. Certain bills go first to Squib. His orders." Tucker tipped his hat to the boy. "Merry Christmas to you and yours!"

In his office, Josiah wrapped a half dozen books. He seemed utterly unperturbed as a highly agitated Rufus burst into the room. "Blast it, Josiah. Half the books have been bound. On time, too! How did that happen?"

An irritable Squib replied, "Control yourself, Rufus. What did you expect me to do? Garrote the binders? I slowed them down as much as I could."

"Not enough, apparently. Our plan's been foiled. And you sit there wrapping presents, you silly goose." Rufus harrumphed, though not convincingly.

Snapped Squib, "Gander, please. You're supposed to know how to use the language. Now, I fail to see what upsets you so. What does it matter if the book has been bound? Where is it going? Not a bookseller in London knows about it, no newspaper will receive a copy. I've seen to that."

Rufus looked out the window. Rain clouds were rolling into London's skies. "If word gets out, the book will sell quickly. That's what you predicted."

Having caught his finger in the ribbon, Squib ripped open one bow in exasperation. "Well, send my crystal ball back to the factory! What do you think I am? An oracle? I'm telling you! The book won't be reviewed by the papers in time for anybody to buy it or the book-sellers to stock it. In the meantime, we spread our own word. Start salting rumors about his defaulting on debts. Act burdened, sympathetic—woebegone, if you will. Now, let's hear it. You can practice on me if you like."

Neither publisher heard the soft thump thump of Newborn's crutch. Ben paused at the sound of voices in the office. He heard Rufus say, "It's not our fault if he ends up in debtors' prison."

Josiah concurred, "You did everything for that man you could, didn't you?"

Ben loitered long enough to hear the scratching of a chair on bare flooring. Squib had stood and was saying, "I thought I would hand-deliver a dozen complimentary copies to Leech."

"Smart move," approved Rufus. "It's his business we want."

Squib's voice grew louder. Nearing his office door, he promised, "I shan't be long."

Ben ducked behind a corner and watched the two men exit Squib's office. He heard the tinkle, thunk as the two men left the building, the front doorbell ringing and the front door slamming. Squib locked the door with a jangle, jangle as he simultaneously complained about the rain.

Ben entered Squib's office, which was small, plain, and bare. No pictures hung on the walls. No carpeting covered the floors. No effects imbued the room with personality of any sort. Using this office as evidence, Ben could deduce little about Squib, his habits, likes, or dislikes.

Ben's eyes scanned the desk, upon which lay a ledger entitled A Christmas Carol. This, Ben picked up and inserted within the binder's last bill. He closed the ledger, tapped a finger on the cover. Something bothered him, he knew not what . . .

Intuition called. Squib had behaved strangely throughout the book's printing, as though he were trying to slow down the process. He had spirited away invoices as soon as they arrived even though they were the business of Charles Dickens. He had mentioned debtors' prison as casually as others would remark upon a haberdasher's. All these factors, Ben considered. They certainly did not point to a logical conclusion.

He looked around the empty office.

His inner voice commanded—move!

He did not think twice.

Ben rifled Squib's desk.

He pawed through the drawers until he found what he suspected. In the lower right-hand drawer Squib kept the phony invoices and bogus ledger for <u>A Christmas Carol</u>. Ben pounced upon the ledger.

The very first entry he recognized. It came from Pimlico Paperworks, but the amount read eighty-nine pounds fifteen shillings. Ben frowned. Hadn't the teamster said fifty-nine? Ben flipped through the ledger's pages. Light dawned. He bent over the desk and ransacked the pile of invoices in the drawer. He stopped at one labeled: "For Incidentals and Advertising, 168 pounds."

Ben reeled. One hundred sixty-eight pounds! A colossal sum! And for what! He'd seen no advertising whatsoever.

Ben's mind raced. Debtors' prison, debtors' prison. They had been talking about . . .

From downstairs wafted the clanking of a key in the front door. Ben froze. Footsteps growing louder.

Ben swiped a copy of the book and pocketed the advertising invoice. As quietly as he could, he tried to shut the desk drawer—but it stuck. He tried again. No luck. The footsteps grew ever louder. By the heavy tread, Ben knew it was Ledrook. Ben had no choice but to leave the drawer ajar.

In the doorway loomed the corpulent publisher. He seemed not terribly surprised upon seeing Ben. "Newborn, what are you doing here? Haven't the others gone?"

Ben, on his crutch, headed for the door. "Tucker asked me to bring up the final sums. I've left them for Mr. Squib."

Ledrook grunted, flashed a glance at the desktop upon which lay the other ledger. Ben dared not look back. He continued out the door with a "Merry Christmas, Mr. Ledrook."

"Yes, merry, you know," he replied.

Using his crutch more for moral than physical support, Ben headed downstairs and straight for the front door. Frustrated again, he found the door locked. Only Ledrook and Squib had keys. Ben tried to force the lock, but the bell only jangled in a dead giveaway of his whereabouts. He bit his lip, turned.

He heard overhead the heavy steps of Ledrook walking in an arc about Josiah's office. Then silence. Ledrook had arrived at his partner's desk. Now the sound of a stuck drawer scraping wide open. Ben, as noiselessly as he knew how, walked to the back door leading to the alley.

The sound of the desk drawer slamming . . . hurried footsteps across the second floor, now down the stairs. Ben grabbed his crutch and headed out the back.

In pouring rain, Ben made his way down the mucky alley. Just around the corner lay the Strand.

Guessing his quarry's route, Rufus exited via the front door and headed for the corner. He would nab the blasted sneak thief and tackle him on the spot. Puff, puff as he chugged along.

At the corner, pursuer and prey ran, smack dab, right into each other. For a second each reeled, but Ben recovered first and took off up the Strand. Cursing to himself, Rufus gave chase, calling as he went, "Stop! Thief!"

Darting about under their umbrellas, the pedestrians really didn't see—or much care—about this chase. What each wanted was a nice, warm hearth and a snifter full of brandy.

Ben's leg hurt. It hadn't hurt this badly since Birmingham. He doubted how long he could stay ahead of Ledrook, who was surprisingly spry given his weight and condition. Ben sneaked a look over his shoulder. He needn't have worried. Rufus Ledrook had somehow tripped and fallen facedown in a gutter. A coach horse nearly stepped on him.

A split second later, Ben saw Paige dart across the street. No doubt she had tripped up the maladroit publisher. Ben would know soon enough. For now, he needed a place to hide. With the trouble he had caused, he could not go back to Alice. Ledrook and Squib might look for him there. He grimaced to think of Alice's shame in hearing that her Benjamin stood accused of theft. No, he could not go home.

Dickens basked in the blessedness of his home. He sat on the floor of the garret and read to his children with great force and feeling:

> "Scrooge looked at the Ghost and with a mournful shaking of his head, glanced anxiously toward the door. The door opened and a little girl, much younger than the boy, came darting in:
>
> 'I have come to bring you home, dear brother!' said the child, clapping her tiny hands . . . "

At that Mamie reached over and grabbed little Charley's hand. For a change, he didn't pull away. Dickens continued:

> " 'To bring you home, home, home! Home for good and all. Home for ever and ever!' "

As the children delighted in the story's end . . .

Ben Newborn found himself, once again, homeless and on the streets of London.

CHAPTER NINE

oodle peered at an envelope lying inside the front door just below the letter drop. With a groan, he bent over and picked it up. The name "Carol Dickens" appeared in neatly penciled letters across the face of the rain-dampened envelope. Boodle dried it by wiping it several times against his sleeve.

Boodle toddled toward the

drawing room, where the entire family had gathered. Everybody spoke at once, the children, Mrs. Dickens, Mrs. Plimpton: "One ghost sounded like Boodle!" "Papa, what's a Fezziwig?" "Is Tiny Tim coming to dinner?" "Marley Farley Charlie Barleycorn!" "Oooh, I'm the Ghost of Christmas Presents!"

Mrs. Dickens, swaddled in a blanket, sat by the fire, happiness fueling her contented features.

Boodle stood by with a salver upon which lay the envelope. Dickens beckoned to his butler, took and opened the communiqué. Quizzical at first, he scanned the enclosure again and again. Then his expression darkened as would a developing tornado. "Where did you find this, Boodle?"

"Under the letter drop, sir."

Catching her husband's ominous tone, Catherine asked, "Is something wrong, Charles?"

"Ah, no dear. Just give me a moment to compose myself. Excuse me."

At the same time, a flushed and excited Carlyle arrived. Catherine welcomed him to the drawing room, where he looked about and blurted out, "Where's Charles! I must speak to him!" In his hand he held a copy of the Carol.

Catherine waved him into the room. "You've read it, I see."

Carlyle came to her side. "He kindly sent me one of the first copies."

Catherine said a short prayer before asking, "And?"

A ruddy-cheeked Carlyle leaned over and said, "He's done it, Catherine! This will outlive us all. Years from now, when no one remembers any of us, the world will remember Cratchit and Tim and Scrooge. They are true because it's the spirit he has captured, the sense of Christmas he has conveyed. It was never meant to be a season of godless revelry but a time to embrace one's unselfish soul. We need to hear this in our mean, dark times. Charles has shown us his light."

Catherine's eyes shone. Carlyle's opinion meant so much to Charles. For once, her husband would hear from this man he revered unstinting, unqualified praise. She was so grateful for this gift of good news that she failed to notice the rainwater Thomas dripped all over the floor. Without prompting, Mrs. Plimpton took his soaking wet coat and umbrella.

Mrs. Dickens clasped his hand and nodded toward the hall. "He's in his study. Go to him. He will be overjoyed, I know!"

Stamping his shoes to shed rain, Thomas headed toward the study door and knocked. "Who is it?" Charles called.

"The other Scrooge! It is I, that cranky, rasty, pessimistic Scot who has come to surrender his soul to you!"

Charles swung open the door. To Carlyle's surprise, his friend looked not at all beatific. No, as Charley ushered Carlyle in and fast shut the door, the creator of Scrooge looked himself as hard and sharp as flint.

"I don't understand," the Scot stammered.

"They're stealing from me, Thomas. I'm sure of it."

"*Who* is stealing from you?"

"Ledcrook and Friends. Look at this! An invoice for advertising and incidentals when there haven't even been any." At this, Charley shoved one bill under his good friend's nose. Once Thomas saw the sum, he gasped. "Ah! You see! It's an astronomical amount," said Charley. "And look at this invoice for paper. Eighty-nine pounds! Yes, I used top-notch stock, but not papyrus handcrafted by the priests of Osiris."

Charles paced while a weak-kneed Carlyle slumped in a wing chair. "Charles, don't leap to any conclusions. Talk with the paper vendor. Gather the facts. Squib has a right to a surcharge."

Charley wasn't even listening, "It all fits. I've always wondered about their bookkeeping—and the so-called slump in my sales. Ha!"

Thomas reproached his friend. "Careful, there! Don't besmirch the good name of that firm. You don't even know who left these documents. They could be fraudulent."

Charley waved one bill in the air. "I know too well Josiah's hand. This is authentic, all right."

"Then who brought it! Answer that!"

Dickens chewed his lip. "I can't. I don't know. Perhaps it was Bob. He might have known the true price of the paper."

"Does he have access to the advertising accounts?" Carlyle remained unconvinced.

Stumped for the moment, Charley could only reply, "No. That's a problem. Only Josiah and Rufus have that."

Carlyle cautioned, "Before you charge off on another Crusade, be sure that you know your friend from your foe."

Dickens ran a hand again and again through his hair, which stood on end, as though the ghost of Marley had appeared at the door. "Who would take the risk of sending me this? And why? My witness is a mystery in more ways than one."

"He'd best be credible. You can't afford to defame a major publisher — not with your career foundering as it is."

"Thank you." Dickens examined the envelope. No clue there. He turned the envelope over and held it to a light. "Hold on! There's a watermark." He picked up a magnifying glass.

Carlyle offered, "It's probably the name of your vendor."

"No, no, it says . . . Aldgate Paperworks."

Both men fell silent. What could this mean? "Did you say Aldersgate?" asked Carlyle.

"No, Aldgate." Aldersgate, Newgate, Ludgate, Ramsgate, names given long ago by Norse settlers of the City. But Aldgate?

Befuddled, Carlyle wondered, "I can understand Aldersgate in the City of London . . . banking, commerce, the lord mayor living there, but Aldgate . . . " His voice trailed off.

Dickens picked up the trail . . . "Way to the east near Petticoat Lane. Absolutely no one respectable dares set a foot there."

"Then how do you know it, Charles?"

"It's safer than St. Giles, and you know I've walked those streets. But Aldgate Paperworks, I've never heard of it."

"What neighborhood is that?"

"Aldgate."

"Oh, stop it, Charles! Is Aldgate in Shoreditch or—"

"Whitechapel. I know the workhouse there. Horrendous!"

Carlyle shook his head. "We're not making any progress. Who in Heaven's name would come from that abode of the damned?"

Dickens looked out his window into the barren little garden. Then he looked again at the envelope. The handwriting was startlingly perfect. Very even. Letters well formed. From the hand of someone taught penmanship properly. "Thomas," he asked, "if one didn't learn a perfect hand at school, where else might one learn it?"

"Well, from a very good governess—or tutor. Or at Sunday school."

"From a churchman? Oh, law, no!" Dickens slapped his forehead.

"Why are you striking yourself?"

"I assumed this fellow addressed me as Carol because he knew the title of my newest book. Perhaps that's not it."

Carlyle rose in a flash. "No! He knows a little Latin . . . and he's letting you know it. What employee of Josiah's would know Latin and live in Aldgate!"

Charles nodded. "I think I know, but I need to be sure."

Carlyle agreed. "You'd better be sure! Too much is at stake, Charles. Move carefully. Mind your manners and your temper, too!"

It was pouring in the morning as the remnants of Roger Knight's gang formed a little circle around a streetlamp. In their midst, an ironworker read aloud a Reward sign posted to the lamp.

"*Reee-waaarð!*" the man trumpeted. "For-tee pounds for in-forma-tion leading to the capture of Benjamin James Newborn, thief, embezzler, forger. See Ledrook and Squib, one eighty-six the Strand!"

Silence. Then the wee mob erupted in whistles, cackles, hoots, their words stumbling over one another's: Yike! Forty pounds! So Ben was a thief! A big-time thief too! Never guessed he had it in him!

As Paige ambled up the lane, the boys ran forward to tell her the news. With her long hair tucked up in her cap, she could still pass for one of them, although probably not for long. Mother Nature was forming on Paige's face delicate, highly feminine features. She might even become a beauty.

At the same time, Charles Dickens read another copy of the flyer, one posted right on the storefront of Ledrook and Squib. For a few seconds, rage ran through his veins, but he made a deliberate decision to cool his blood. He must not tip his hand just yet. He carefully composed his features in as convincing a smile as he could fake.

"Good morning!" Dickens chirped upon entering the building. In the front room, Squib bustled about, stacking copies of <u>A Christmas Carol</u>. He chirped right back, "Oh, good morning to *you*, Charles Dickens!"

Their chirping done, Dickens cut to the quick of their meeting. "I see from the flyer that you're short an employee today."

Looking martyred, Josiah replied, "Oh, yes. That. Terrible. We caught him last night, the little guttersnipe, stealing from my desk. So much for trying to improve the lower classes, eh?"

Reining in his temper, Dickens surveyed the shelves. "Well, well, don't they look ducky. You've worked so hard to spread word of my work! I suppose the advertising invoice will reflect your endless labors on my behalf."

Without missing a beat, Squib exclaimed, "Absolutely! Nothing's too good for Cratchit and Company!"

"And of course you've spread word to the poor, for whom I priced the book so low." Charles smiled.

Josiah smiled right back at him. "Done! Just what poor people need, too! Leather-bound printings for their private libraries!"

Charles choked on a snarl and snatched a dozen copies from the desktop. "Ta, Josiah."

"Good day, Charles!" Josiah waved at the departing author his goose-feather duster. Once the door closed behind Charley, Josiah said gleefully to no one in particular, "Good-*bye*, Mr. Dickens."

With the small volumes easily tucked under one arm, Dickens stormed up the Strand. He muttered to himself all the way up Fleet Street and past St. Paul's, the Bank of England, the Royal Exchange and Stock Exchange. This was the heart of ancient London and the cradle of her financial future. Ironically, it lay but blocks away from the direst straits of the City. Behind the back of the Old Lady of Threadneedle Street, London starved and stole and succumbed to disease.

Dickens strode along to Aldgate Hill and stopped. If he turned right, the Tower of London lay but five blocks away. If he turned left, he could cut through Stoney Lane to Petticoat Lane, thronged with vendors selling all sorts of wares — many of them not even stolen. Left, Dickens did turn and wended his way along the narrow streets to . . .

Whitechapel. Strangely, the bedizened Dickens did not attract any pickpockets—or worse. Quite the opposite. Many passersby nodded or smiled at this familiar character. They knew on sight the creator of <u>Oliver Twist</u> and they respected him, left him alone. He was one bloke from the fancy side of town who spoke their language, knew their anguish. He had revealed in <u>Twist</u> an intimacy with the ways and wiles of street people and the hardness of their lives.

Once on Petticoat Lane, Dickens readily found a bookseller he knew and hurried to speak with the old Cockney buzzard. His name was Toobie and he leaned to one side. There was no reason for this. One leg wasn't any shorter than the other; he hadn't lost hearing in one or the other of his ears. He just leaned to one side, like a sailor stuck on a portside roll.

Dickens showed Toobie the book and explained the dual purpose of his call. Awed by the beauty of the volume, Toobie could hardly believe his eyes or ears. "This beauty costs five bob?"

"Right. And if you find Ben Newborn for me, I'll give you an entire box of them."

Toobie, like the raven in the garden, looked askance at Dickens. "Now, why should I know this Newborn fellow? You tell me that, sir, you tell me that. How should I know this boy Benjamin?"

Dickens played along. "Uh-huh. How many adolescent males in this neighborhood would buy your <u>Bentley's Miscellany</u>?"

"What makes you think he buys, not steals them? You tell me that, sir. You tell me that."

Dickens forced himself to take a deep breath. "Are you saying you have never seen nor heard of the Newborn lad?"

The dealer thought, pursed his lips. "Supposing I had, supposing I had. What should I say to him if I had?"

"You tell him to go straightaway to my home. Got that?"

"It's not exactly hard to remember, sir." He paused briefly before asking, "Just where is your home?"

"Oh, he knows. Somehow, he knows. Do we have a deal?"

They shook hands, the Cockney rightening himself by a few degrees in the process. Dickens gave Toobie the books and walked away. As though on cue, Paige sidled up to the bookseller. She asked defensively, "He wanted Ben, didn't he?"

The Cockney bobbed his head. "An oracle you are, my child."

"Well, don't trust him! He'd turn Ben in."

Toobie laughed. "I don't thinks Dickens needs the reward money, do you?"

Paige parried, "What if he did? What if he really was broke?"

Toobie riposted immediately, "I know somebody who could use the money—you! You been tearing down all those reward signs. Going ta keep the money for yourself?" Paige didn't answer, so the sly bustard asked, "You knows where he is, don't you?"

"If I did, you'd be the last to know!" She taunted.

Toobie clicked his tongue, tsk tsk. "No reason for you not to trust me, girl. I'm just a curious chap. I like things neat and clear." He suspended his makeshift work and gave her a critical stare. "How you'd know what flyers to tear down when you can't even read?"

Flummoxed, Paige opened her mouth but was saved when an ostler interrupted them both. He greeted Toobie cheerfully. "Mornin', guv'ner! I'll have a copy of <u>The Times</u>."

Toobie gave the laborer a hard look. "You reading the financial news these days?"

"Nope." The ostler shook his head. "I need to wrap up me fish."

As Toobie fetched <u>The Times</u>, Paige sneaked away.

That evening, not only night fell. What descended upon London surprised Dickens in his tracks. Like angel-strewn confetti, snow fell from the heavens, flakes landing intact upon the hard-packed earth. Snow rarely fell in London at that time of year, and Charles hadn't thought the ground cold enough to hold it. It was. In spite of his woes, the sight coaxed a grin from Charley.

The unexpected flurries reduced adults on the street to childlike wonder. Many left work that night laughing, grasping at flakes as though they were manna. The powder tickled the noses of coach horses who sneezed on the passersby.

Throughout the evening, snow dusted the City, transforming gray horizons into comforters of white. The docks, yards, and gardens of London appeared as though purified, cleansed, and renewed.

Dickens stared at his own garden, the bare branches garbed in snow white and frost. Catherine entered, saw her husband frozen in contemplation by the garden door. She walked to him, commenting softly, "It's lovely, isn't it? A Christmas counterpane of snow."

"More like a shroud," Dickens replied.

A mantel clock ticked too loudly. Almost offhand, Catherine asked, "How much longer before your good watch is fixed? It's been, what . . . two months now?"

Dickens patted her hand. "The wrong part arrived by post. Not much longer, dear."

Despite the chill and damp, Ben sat outside on a walkway some 360 feet above ground. By torchlight, he strained to read. With one hand he held a little book. With the other he shielded the torch from a stiff breeze off the river.

His features constricted as he read to himself:

They went, the Ghost and Scrooge, across the hall, to a door at the back of the house. It opened before them, and disclosed a long, bare, melancholy room, made barer still by lines of plain deal forms and desks. At one of these a lonely boy was reading near a feeble fire; and Scrooge sat down upon a form and wept to see his poor forgotten self as he had used to be . . . and wept to see his poor forgotten self as he had used to be . . . and wept to see . . .

Ben couldn't continue. He kept tripping over these last words which echoed time after time in his mind.

He put the book down and stared ahead. He could just perceive in the lingering dusk the Tower of London's twenty turrets, many lit now by torches. It was all in there, locked from sight, the desperate last hours of queens and kings, saints and spies, princes and pretenders . . . an endless procession of once powerful people harboring the very same terror of death as a commoner caught stealing bread.

The formidable fortress, medieval Europe's largest, seemed not so very terrifying these nights. It was home now to the crown jewels, the beefeater guards, and a flock of wing-clipped ravens. Its vast, menacing, blackwater moat, dug half a century before, no longer encircled the stronghold. A spawning ground for cholera, the moat had been drained earlier in the year under the direction of the duke of Wellington.

Ben studied this vista with all of his own and formidable powers. Having steeped himself in his nation's history, he appreciated what he saw. Little was ever wasted on Benjamin Newborn.

He understood this—he was himself standing at a crossroads of gravest consequence. He or Dickens or perhaps the two of them were facing prison—Newgate for Ben, the Marshalsea for Charles.

However, one major difference distinguished their fates. Dickens might spend gaol time for his debts, wasting away for a matter of months.

For thieving, Ben's imprisonment would last two days, after which he would be taken out and hanged.

In the nightscape of Ben's mind, the Tower loomed ever larger.

CHAPTER TEN

here Ben Newborn
had taken refuge,
only Paige knew.

She darted inside
St. Paul's Cathe-
dral just as a curate locked its massive
side doors. Within, the building rose
as a sunburst of beauty in wrought
iron, carved stone, and gold. Oblivious to the magnificence all about her,
Paige scurried along the nave to a
flight of stairs. As fit as she was, she

handily climbed the 259 steps from the cathedral floor to the Whispering Gallery. Here, at the base of the dome, paintings depicted episodes in the life of St. Paul, but Paige ignored these, too. She had no way to know what they meant. She also had 271 more steps to go—straight up and through the dizzying heights of the Stone and Golden Galleries.

The steps wound round and round, up and away from the cathedral floor to the sky and heaven above. As Paige ascended the very last flight, her leg muscles began to hurt. Just as she felt a spasm in one leg, Paige arrived at the summit of the dome. Sweating despite the chill, she stepped out into a world with London at its feet, the river for a red carpet, the Tower for a throne. Torches flickered throughout the City, fireflies of light in the falling night. The breathtaking view came after a breathtaking climb. Paige needed a minute to catch her wind. As she did, she heard Ben say, "Up here, I can hear my mother singing."

Paige's eyes adjusted to the dusk and discerned Benjamin waiting by the railing. He wore still his flimsy old jacket. Paige shook her head. "You can't stay here tonight. You'll freeze," she said, handing Ben a chunk of brown bread.

Ben snatched the bread with one hand but clutched in the other his copy of <u>A Christmas Carol</u> and a small, cardboard folio. "That the last of the gold leaf?" Paige asked.

Between gulps of bread, Ben said, "I can't give it to you."

Thinking that Ben joked, Paige scoffed. "After a climb like that, you better. I come a long, long way for the last of that leaf."

Ben moved away. "It is not mine to give you."

Paige paused, unsure that Ben meant business. She took a moment to regain her mental balance, then forged ahead. "Alice is better. Why would you think of stopping now?"

Ben repeated very slowly, "It is not mine to give you."

Paige's features darkened. Unamused, she protested, "Judas Priest, you knew from the start you was stealing. I can understand your havin' a pang or two, but look at the good you're doing. And she's askin' for you, Ben. What are you going to tell her? No more medicine? Sorry?"

Ben stared out onto the vista below as though he were oblivious to it all. "I'll tell her nothing. I won't be seeing her again."

Paige, her arches cramping, did not want to argue this time. "I don't care, Newborn. We had an understandin'."

Ben turned to give her his best glower, but his eyes softened. The girl had grown several inches since they had first met. Though gaunt, she displayed hints of haunting beauty in her haughty face and carriage. Most arresting were her enormous blue eyes, deep-set in a pale face and flashing like sapphires whenever backlit by deep emotion. Taken aback, Ben sounded a bit tentative in saying, "You've got to promise me something. If I end up in gaol—"

Paige, flapping her arms to keep warm, cut him off. "You're not going to Newgate! I took care of the reward posters. Wasn't easy, either. All I could figure was the number forty and the pound sign. Law, what a job! As for those publishers, forget 'em. Ditherin' idiots, if you ask me."

"Listen to me!" Ben shouted.

"I won't! I won't!" Paige walked straight into Benjamin's face. "I went out on a limb for you. Don't you double-cross me." In suspecting betrayal, Paige masked hurt with fury.

Ben wouldn't budge. "You're getting this all wrong. Listen to me. You know what the penalty is for thieving, and they've called me an embezzler, too. Maybe they're pretending I stole some money. In this whole mess, I can reckon just one thing. I lost my own family, but I can help another one. I have to do it, but I need a miracle. Only one person can work that miracle, a person who has a duty to send me to prison,"

Paige grabbed Ben by the shoulders. "Then don't let the blighter near you! Get ahold of yourself, Ben! I lost me family, too. You seen it for yourself."

Being so close to Paige, Ben felt paralyzed, a new sensation. He would not, however, relent. "I know,

Paige, but the police can't help us, not about Roger. They'd never believe a word you said about his defending you. And what good is my word now? I just want you to promise that if I end up at Newgate, you'll never tell Alice. It would kill her. You know it would."

Panic flooded Paige's brain. Her breathing grew irregular, her eyes widened unnaturally. "No," she quietly repeated again and again. She clasped the rusty railing, all that stood between the two of them and the pavement thirty-six stories below.

. . . Then footsteps on the staircase leading to the gallery. Ben grabbed her free arm and pointed a finger in her face. "Swear to me on the grave of your brother. Not a word to Alice about what I've done!"

The footsteps paused, the door handle rattled. "Come on, Paige, give me your word. I've got no more time."

Paige, tears of frustration welling in her beautiful eyes, looked skyward, cut loose with a wail. At the same instant, who should poke his head through the door but the bookseller Toobie, panting and sweating heavily. "I thought you'd be here! Come on, boy, I'll give you a hideout, one warmer than this, I tell you. Whew!"

Worn-out by his climb, Toobie leaned against the far railing and tried to recover his breath. Each of the three traded glances with the others, but nobody moved. Paige, alarmed and confused, could only ask lamely, "You followed me. Why?"

Ignoring Paige, Toobie looked to Ben. "That Dickens

151

fellow wants to help you. Right nice chap, he is. Come on, then. We'll go to his house, just you and me."

Ben raised his voice. "If I know where he lives, why would I need you to take me there?"

Paige sucked in her breath. She turned away, knowing that she had given away Ben's sanctuary.

Toobie's eyelids lowered, his grin spread. "Heh, heh. Just where do you think you're goin', Ben? White-chapel's crawlin' with coppers. Half the neighborhood wants to turn you in, forty pounds not exactly bein' hay, if you know what I mean. Where can you go? Who can you trust but me?"

"Maybe he's right, Ben—" Paige said, but Toobie, baying like a bloodhound, cut her off.

Paige pivoted, but . . . the boy was gone. Vanished into thin air. Paige looked about wildly, scanning the towers, spires, skyline. Toobie, transfixed, stared at the railing where Ben had stood. Gathering her courage, Paige looked straight down. Sweet Mother of Jesus, there was Ben—lowering himself by rope down the dome, his crutch looped over a shoulder! Paige couldn't believe her eyes. This was asking for death, especially with the dome so slippery from freshly fallen snow.

Paige clutched her skull. Everything had gone wrong. She had lost the only family she had known—her brother. She had come to realize that Ben himself was her only hope, her heart, her happiness—the one person in the world she cherished or for whom she could feel any tenderness. Now he had abandoned her, too.

"Ben!" screamed Paige, but the wind whipped her words away.

"Well, I'll be!" muttered Toobie as Benjamin landed hard on the roof, then clambered away into the dark.

The wind picked up, moaning as it flowed like a formless ghost through the cathedral's towers. Paige wanted to flee. As she headed for the door, Toobie grabbed her left elbow. "You come with me, girl. I knows what's good for you."

She looked into his eyes and read in them an expression she had never before seen. She did not like it at all. She pulled away from Toobie, but he held fast. She jerked her arm hard, but he held her tightly, his smile transforming into a leer. "Let me go!" she demanded. Toobie only laughed and roughly pulled her toward him.

The door flung open. A black-cassocked young curate, key ring rattling in hand, poked his head through. "Closing time! You'll need to be going!"

Paige's eyes pleaded with the curate, no fool he. Before him stood a panic-stricken young lady and a rough-hewn scalawag with a tight grip on her arm.

Toobie gave the intruder his most gracious grin. "She and me, we were just on our way . . . "

The curate smiled just as graciously. "Oh, I don't

think so! She promised me earlier help with the poor box!"

Paige, the sneak thief, gaped. Toobie's grin collapsed. "But . . . "

"No buts. Come, child!" As though shooing away a stray cat, the young man waved at Toobie. "Off with you, now!" The cleric placed himself between Toobie and Paige so that the girl might get away safely.

Livid, Toobie plodded down the stairs. With half the neighborhood looking for the boy, the bookseller knew he'd lost his chance of nabbing Ben.

The snow fell sparingly throughout the night, making of Carlyle's garden a wonderland in miniature. Here the historian enjoyed a pipe as he ruminated upon events of the day. He had to admit, Charles Dickens might be right. Perhaps adults needed a season of being children, a chance to purify and renew the human heart. Reborn, regenerated for the rigors of winter, the human soul might fly more lightly through its darker hours and times.

Come to me as little children—that summed up Dickens, Carlyle thought. Because Charley himself still harbored the heart of a child—impetuous, overflowing, wonder-struck—he could be reborn in any given year, at any Christmastide, in any tale he chose to tell. Carlyle wondered if others might do the same. Perhaps this season would again achieve a significance beyond roasting Yule logs and turkeys, or eating and wassailing oneself silly, like those revelers of merry old England.

He reflected upon Cromwell, whose Parliament had damned those revelers, banned their wintertide customs and festivities at Christmas. What would the Lord Protector think if he knew that two-hundred years later, his biographer might actually embrace this whole Christmas business? Harrumph. Humbug. As much as he admired Cromwell, Carlyle decided that the Lord Protector had erred on this matter.

No, Charley had made of this season a time for the giving of the hidden self. May God bless him, bless us, concluded Carlyle in a state of heretofore unexperienced calm.

Ironically, Charles at that time enjoyed no such bliss, tossing and turning in his sleep. He could not block out the voices that haunted him — his father, Squib, Ledrook, and Cromwell. They formed a conspiracy of naysayers who found him a fool, a fool for wanting the unattainable. A Heavenly Kingdom could never be forged where greed and deceit ruled the human heart. Whoever thought otherwise was naive, silly, daft.

Tired from fitful sleep, Dickens awakened to see a

wizened, clawlike hand clinging to his bedpost. He shook his head. He saw then looming at the foot of his bed a tall, thin figure dressed in black. "Cromwell!" he called out.

His discombobulated butler stared back at him. "The name is Boodle, sir." He sighed at being forgotten.

Ben had trod the walkway of power—Whitehall. Here loomed one faceless gray structure after another, the buildings of British government. In the dim light of dawn, these gargantuan formations looked like a cortege of elephants making their way to age-old burial grounds—solemn, silent, huge.

In the dark, Ben had stolen down the Strand, then turned south onto Whitehall, a boulevard. The area took its name from a mansion named White Hall, once the grand home of King Henry VIII. Yet long, long before, another grand palace had stood on the spot. The English King Edgar gave this Gothic prize to the Scottish King Kenneth so that his court might have lodging whenever it visited London. For nine hundred years, through several transformations, through the burning and wrecking of the palace in 1698, one site retained its original association. At 4 Whitehall Place, the passerby found not a second home for Scotland's kings but the home of Prime Minister Robert Peel's police. Just as these "bobbies" borrowed a nickname from their founder, they borrowed another nickname for their workplace—Scotland Yard.

Ben passed 4 Whitehall Place en route to his destination. He sought a plain, unimpressive place, a house erected long ago as the home of a former ambassador to the Netherlands. Surrounded by the mammoths of imperial business, this house looked like a neighborhood intruder. Its builder: Sir George Downing. Its street number: 10. Its occupants: prime ministers.

Here Ben bided his time, hiding in an alley across the street. He observed a milkman and costermonger delivering goods, stepping down to the cellar kitchens. Number 10 had started to stir. At last a liveried butler stepped outside the front door and regarded with dismay the snow-laden stoop. Within a minute, the butler was directing footmen who quickly cleared the walkway. Satisfied with the job of his underlings, the butler retired inside.

Ben said a prayer to himself, then walked across the street. This time he leaned on his crutch as though his life depended upon it. Never had his leg hurt this badly. He had strained it in climbing to the top of St. Paul's. He had landed too hard on the cathedral roof. The cold of the night hadn't helped. His muscles badly needed warmth and rest, not cold and stress.

He arrived at the door of No. 10. So rigid were his fingers, it took considerable effort to grasp the brass knocker. Yet the chill that reduced him to shivers came not from cold but fear.

The front door swung open. The liveried butler

looked out—and right over Ben's head. Newborn solemnly intoned, "I have come to see Sir Robert Peel."

Incredulous, the butler looked straight at Ben as though the boy were a circus freak. He thought for a moment—then tried to slam the door in Ben's face. Anticipating this prospect, the lad quickly thrust his crutch in the doorjamb, blocking the butler's move. He said very evenly, "I have the right to petition my prime minister. I come to him in the name of those who died in Birmingham, in the disaster at the iron mines. You come back here and tell me he has said no to those victims. You come back here and tell me he won't listen to the story of Tess, my sister killed in the explosion. You come back here and tell me that he doesn't care to pass legislation that could have saved my parents. I've got something to say to him and I'll say it to him *now*!"

Ben's quiet passion, his undiminished resolve, deeply moved the butler. He said nothing but indicated for Ben to wait. Then he shut the door.

Ben caved in on his crutch. Then they started—the coughs, coughs so deep they wracked his frame. Coughs that sounded just like those that ravaged Alice's body. Ben's face, skeletally pale and tinged with blue, barely conveyed the hope of life.

The door reopened. The butler, his eyes sad, looked down at Ben. It took him several seconds to muster a calm voice and say, "The prime minister will see you in the library."

. . .

Exhausted, Ben trailed the butler down a labyrinth of hallways. It was so warm within, so safe, so beautiful. As tired as he felt, Ben still ogled the gleaming Georgian silver, the lustrous Devonshire china, the elegant Regency chairs that graced No. 10. He had never seen anything like these appointments in his life and wondered where they came from, what one might call them.

They made little noise as they walked along, their footsteps muffled by wine-red rugs. The butler finally stopped by an open door and gestured for Ben to enter that room.

This, Ben did, but halted in his tracks. On three sides the library was lined with floor-to-ceiling bookshelves, their burnished hardwoods basking in firelight. Flames in the hearth beat away the gloom. By the fire sat a lady and gentleman enjoying their morning coffee.

Agape, Ben finally noticed that the man had arisen and was coming toward him; Ben's brain started to fail. He was so overcome by the wealth of volumes housed in this one room, and the beauty and light that suffused the scene with grace, that his mind and mouth went their separate ways. He could not speak. He could not even think.

Sir Robert looked even more handsome when viewed up close than at a distance. Intelligence shone in his sea-blue eyes. He said nothing to Ben but motioned for him to approach. Now the lady by the fire looked politely at Ben. In return, he sneaked a glance at her and his heart did a somersault. Never in his life had he seen such a beautiful woman. It was all too much.

Sir Robert spoke with unexpected candor. "I know what it is to lose someone dear in the line of work. In January I lost my friend, my confidant, my invaluable secretary, Edmund Drummond. He was shot. He died. The assassin's bullet was actually meant for me."

Taken aback, Ben could think of nothing sensible or sympathetic to say. He could not imagine why anyone would want to kill this gracious man. He stammered, "But . . . but why?"

Sir Robert replied politely but in brief. "I clung to my beliefs and Mr. Drummond paid for them. That was an injustice I will never forget. Now, young man, about your business."

Ben retrieved from his jacket the contraband tucked inside—the copy he had stolen of <u>A Christmas Carol</u>. He knew very well to whom he was handing over this purloined copy. No one in the kingdom stood more for law enforcement than the knight whom Benjamin Newborn faced.

Sir Robert opened the book and scanned the title page. His eyebrows rose in surprise. Then he quickly thumbed through the text. "However did you get this? Who are you?" he asked.

Ben could only croak, "My name is Benjamin James Newborn. I was a printer's apprentice."

Sir Robert exchanged a glance with Lady Julia Peel.

"It's a new work by Charles Dickens about which I've heard not a word."

The lady stood and walked to one shelf. "Approach, Master Newborn. You might enjoy the sight of these!" To Benjamin's rapture, the shelf was stocked with books by Dickens: <u>Oliver Twist</u>, <u>Old Curiosity Shop</u>, <u>Nicholas Nickleby</u>, <u>Pickwick Papers</u>—even <u>Martin Chuzzlewit</u>! To his humiliation, tears slid down Benjamin's face, so terrible was his exhaustion, so vast and deep his relief. Prime Minister Peel did like the writings of Mister Dickens!

Mission accomplished, Ben pulled from his pocket a battered flyer folded in four. He was not even afraid as he handed it to the prime minister. Sir Robert unfolded the paper, his expression instantaneously changed. He looked thunderous, like Zeus in learning of a misdeed on Olympus.

He held up to his wife the Reward poster with the name Benjamin James Newborn printed in block letters. Her hand flew to her cheek. The lad in their library was wanted for felonies.

Ben looked Sir Robert straight in the eye, then slowly raised his crutch with both hands. With dignity fit for a squire, Newborn surrendered unto his knight his "sword" and his soul, his body unto the law.

It was a beautiful, brisk, sun-blessed December day. Josiah Squib whistled as he set about opening the shop and reception area. Through the bay window he glimpsed a barouche rumbling to a stop right at the storefront. It was a magnificent carriage pulled by a team of exactly matched Hackneys. Josiah rubbed his hands. Somebody rich was coming to the shop!

The little bell over the front door tinkled. Into the front room then swooped a fabulously handsome lady — upper crust to the core, dressed in the finest bonnet and matching wool greatcoat. To this female wonder, Josiah oozed, "Good morning, m'lady. Whom may I say I have the pleasure of serving today?"

"Good morning, sir. I am Lady Julia Peel. No doubt you've heard of my husband, Sir Robert." Julia delivered this with the authority of a general's daughter — which she was.

Josiah tried not to swoon as he wondered what fortune had brought to his door the wife of the kingdom's prime minister. "I am honored, your ladyship!"

He broke off as another fine carriage, a landau, pulled up to the shop and stopped. Three exquisitely attired women alit and entered, their petticoats rustling like falling leaves in a breeze. Lady Julia greeting each. "Rosalind! Eleanor! Elizabeth! Thank you for answering my notes."

Josiah felt himself heaven-borne on bags of money. Here were four of the noblest women he had ever hoped to see, and certainly never in his humble store.

Lady Julia nodded to a stack of books behind his

back. "That new volume by Mister Charles Dickens. What does it cost?"

Josiah did not register the question. Surely he had heard incorrectly. "Ah, certainly your ladyship is not interested in this, this, well, whatever it is this is. We have a fine selection of new titles suited to your ladyship's no doubt exquisite sensibilities."

"How much?" she shot back.

"Ah, ah, ten shillings."

Her perfectly arched eyebrows rose in amusement. "I was told five shillings!"

Josiah slapped the counter. "Ha! Well, surely . . . " And his voice dropped to a thinly disguised hiss. "Who told you that?"

"Does it matter? Now, I should like to purchase—" and her eyes roamed over the stacks "—twenty copies to start."

"Twenty!" Josiah exclaimed, then excused himself.

The cherubic-faced Rosalind chimed in, "I shall need thirty at the least!"

Eleanor, who had missed her calling to the convent, upped the ante: "The archbishop has such expectations of the volume that no fewer than forty copies will meet His Excellency's requirements."

Josiah leaned on the counter for support. Elizabeth, a bit hard of hearing, spoke too loudly. "I shall need my copies delivered no later than tomorrow. Can you do that, eh? What do you say? Speak up. I can't hear you! What?"

Josiah yelled, "But of course! To what address?"

Elizabeth frowned. "St. James's Palace, of course!"

Josiah bared his teeth and smiled. "Naturally!"

Lady Julia volunteered, "The duke of Wellington and my husband are such dear friends. We told him straightaway of this new book, so I shall be acquiring copies for His Grace as well. Oh, I almost forgot, my husband's new protégés—William and Benjamin!"

"Have they last names, your ladyship?"

With a killing smile, Lady Julia answered, "Gladstone and Disraeli."

The other ladies buzzed with names of persons who they thought should see the book: the duke of Devonshire! The count D'Orsay! The prince Albert! Lady Blessington! Lady Holland! Thackeray, Browning, Balzac! Anyone know Tennyson?

"My lucky day!" Josiah Squib beamed, feeling his stomach surge with the first symptoms of dyspepsia.

CHAPTER ELEVEN

homas Carlyle received a surprise when he presented himself that noon at the publisher's front door. He had intended to buy a few copies of Charley's book and give them to friends as Yuletide tokens. However, a queue had formed at No. 186 the Strand and snaked its way up the avenue. Those waiting on line were, for the most part, well

dressed, but their ranks were peopled with laborers and mongers. Many clucked and cooed over the Wanted posters for Newborn taped to the windows and lampposts.

Confused by the small crowd, Carlyle then spied two vaguely familiar faces—the ladies who had swooned over Dickens after his speech at Parliament and pressed him hard for autographs. With a tip of his top hat, Carlyle approached the ladies and reintroduced himself. He then, to his amazement, learned the purpose of the queue. Everyone had come to buy copies of <u>A Christmas Carol</u>.

Carlyle could not contain his amazement. "This is all just so . . . je ne sais quoi!" Never in his life had Carlyle felt pleased to join a line and wait patiently for it to move.

Within the shop itself, all hands pitched in to help at the counter. Philobuster and Bob ran back and forth from the printer's shack, hauling carton after carton of books to the front. While Tucker sold the copies and counted the change, Josiah and Rufus bickered and dickered.

At No. 10 Downing Street, Lady Julia wrapped her books in green tissue papers and tied them with scarlet ribbons. One package, however, sat by itself. This item was wrapped in fine green linen and tied with a ribbon of silk. Lady Julia handed it to her butler.

By the front door, a yeoman of the Queen's Household Cavalry waited on horseback. The butler scurried from No. 10 and handed the uniformed rider the package. On his massive black horse, the yeoman trotted off with a clop, clop, clop back down Whitehall and onto Birdcage Walk. The plume on his helmet swung in rhythm to the beat of his horse's gait. To his right spread St. James's Park.

So old was the recorded history of the park that it had been noted in the Domesday Book of William the Conqueror. Down through the centuries it had changed hands, from Westminster's abbots to the Tudor and Stuart kings. It was Charles II who had made of it a miniature Eden, a refuge for birds, a trysting place for lovers. He had borrowed from Versailles a landscape designer who had laid out its lakes and pools and canals. Thenceforth it was a tantalizing slice of paradise, a sweep of green with squadrons of swans, the promise of peace and a hint of bliss set in the slate-gray cityscape of London.

The cavalier rode to the end of the enchanted walk, trotted right, and stopped at a gate. His short ride had brought him to Buckingham Palace.

At the same time, Carlyle trotted to a stop at One Devonshire. An excellent equestrian, Thomas could negotiate handily on horseback London's thronged, unpaved, pitted, and perilous streets. He tied up his favorite hack horse then took the steps two at a time.

In minutes, he held Catherine in his thrall. He told her all about the excitement at the publisher's, about the crowd waiting expectantly to buy the book. "Catherine, I don't know how it happened. People are lining up. Polite society is buying it, the poor can buy it. It's, it's . . . a wonder!"

Catherine did indeed look wonder-struck. Shaking her head, she admitted, "I can't believe it. You know our luck in business of late. How did this happen? How did so many learn of the book so fast? I can't find a word of it in any of our newspapers!"

"Strange, that!" muttered Carylyle. "I've seen not a word either. What could Rufus and Josiah have been thinking?"

A loud bang startled them both. Carlyle opened the front door to find on her stoop Bartholomew Bane. This time Catherine was actually glad to see the banker. "Mr. Bane! Something wonderful has happened. You must give us just another week."

Bane pulled from his pocket a document and handed that to Catherine. It was a statement declaring that their house payments had been made—*all of them*. Catherine couldn't grasp this development. "Mr. Bane, I don't understand."

Far from happy, Bane looked thwarted, his upper lip twisted and twitching. "Neither do I. However, it seems that an admirer of your husband's (cough, cough) has chosen to keep for the indefinite future the roof over your head."

"What!" exclaimed Catherine and Thomas at the very same instant.

Bane, eyes wide as an owl's caught in a lantern, complained, "My sentiments exactly! Who, I mean who, possessed of his senses and higher faculties of reasoning would extend such an offer and *insist* on anonymity!"

"What!" exclaimed Catherine and Thomas.

"But you repeat yourselves. I, on the other hand, must assume that your benefactor is a person of misguided sensibilities who has confused the ennobled impulse of charity with the better interests of our expanding empire, for if everybody gave, what would become of our banks? You see my point. Good day, Mrs. Dickens—and whoever you are!" With that, Bane retreated down the steps.

Catherine, uncharacteristically, made a face behind the departing Bane and grumbled to Carlyle, "Humbug!"

Then Charley bounded up the steps and through the door, bumping into Bane, whom he neither recognized nor acknowledged. Without saying a word, he stormed by his wife and startled friend. "Charles!" Catherine offered. "It's paid! Our house payments are paid—in full!"

Carlyle contributed his own cheer. "Your book is selling like hot chestnuts in winter. It's a great, a huge success!"

. . . No comment as Charley disappeared into his study, shutting the door behind him. Catherine looked at her friend. Thomas could only shrug and offer, "Don't look at me. I never did understand him."

She gave him *that* look, the look that said, *Go to my husband and fathom what he is thinking as he keeps from me the truth of our woes*. Thomas shook his head. "Oh, no, Catherine. I don't even want to know what is going on in that mind of his. It's too confusing."

Wordless, she pointed to the study door and gave Thomas a hard look. He sighed and shuffled off like one of her children ordered to his room.

In the study, Dickens paced and raced his fingers through his hair. A timorous Carlyle stuck his head through the door. "Come in and close the door," Dickens directed. "I don't want anyone but you hearing this."

"Lucky me," muttered Carlyle, closing the door behind him.

"I know what you're thinking, but I must explain," said Charles. "Those books are selling on the inflated invoices. They're not adding to my earnings. They're adding to my debts. You see, it's been set up for me to lose on each copy. So the greater the sales, the greater the losses. This edition could spell my ruin. That's why I'm not out there spreading word about my book. How any of this happened, I have no idea!"

With a moan, Carlyle sank into a chair. "Oh, I give up. We never seem to get ahead on this, do we?"

Charley's eyes looked wild. "How long have I been cheated? Did my other books really stop selling? Or have I never seen the true royalties and commissions I have earned?"

Carlyle snapped his fingers. "What about that Aldgate fellow? Your mystery witness?"

Dickens shook his head vigorously. "He seems to have vanished. If the authorities find him first, he'll go to Newgate, depend upon it."

Carlyle looked astonished. "Don't tell me. You're depending on a rogue as your witness?"

"I'm not sure."

Light dawned for Thomas. "Dear me, your publisher posted notice for a real rapscallion—that Newborn boy."

"Same chap," said Charles without expression.

"Heaven help us! You jest!"

"Am I laughing?"

"What will you do?" Carlyle looked more alarmed than did Dickens.

"What I know how to do. Search the streets of London." Sorrow more than anger dimmed the light in Charley's eyes.

Dickens confronted the edifice he detested above all. It actually consisted of four buildings delimiting a square. Its four sides abutted the Old Bailey, the College of Physicians, the Sessions House, and Newgate Street. Here rose the wards of a prison that had haunted Charley since his youth.

As a homeless child en route to the factory, Dickens often passed Newgate Prison. It compelled and repelled him at the same time. He had seen its condemned men hanging in the press-yard next to the ordinary's house on Newgate Street. He had wondered about the crimes committed by the men twisting in the winds that blew in from the river.

As an adult, Charles had returned to this territory and sought to reconquer it, this time as a writer. His journalistic nose had taken him through virtually every cranny of the place, which he had described in detail for <u>The Morning Chronicle</u>. He knew its inmates, male and female. He knew its condemned, wardens, and hangmen. Where in this massive installation might he find the lost likes of a Benjamin Newborn?

Unsure of Ben's age, he visited the school prison for boys under fourteen; Newborn wasn't there. The boys who were looked like creatures from a netherworld that knew neither sun nor love, the souls on their faces absolute blanks upon which the word *hope* would never be written. Charley recollected what he had penned for the paper:

> It is strange with how little notice, good, bad, or indifferent, a man may live and die in London. He awakens no sympathy in the breast of any single person; his existence is a matter of interest to no one save himself; he cannot be said to be forgotten when he dies for no one remembered him when he was alive.

The nerve in Charley's cheek began to burn. He needed to find Newborn. It was no longer a question of

Ben's helping Dickens. It was a question of keeping that precious lad from a bottomless fall into oblivion. Dickens couldn't save every boy at Newgate, but there was one he must and should save from the city streets just as surely as he had needed rescue from the nightmare of his own childhood.

Most horrifically, Dickens knew what would happen if Ben were apprehended and brought to court. At that thought, a tremor shot through Charley's shoulders. He hastened his departure from Newgate.

He tore through Old Bailey and the law courts across the street, buttonholing beadles and sheriffs, describing Ben again and again. No one had seen or heard of anybody by Newborn's name or description. No case against him appeared on any docket.

If Newborn were arrested, he would be brought before a bench in these courts. However, the magistrate's chief duty lay not in presiding over Ben's case but in finding evidence to prove it. Sealing his own doom, the accused did not have the right to speak on his own behalf. Ben had no chance in these courts to protest the false accusations against him.

An anxious Dickens walked miles and miles that day—all the way to Seven Dials and Whitechapel, quizzing anyone who owned or ran a newstand. Ben read well. He sometimes used a crutch. Unfortunately, no one had seen Ben—or would admit that he had. Truly at his wits' end, Dickens wandered down to the river and ransacked his brain, normally a hothouse of solutions to problems. Falling night curtailed his vision but honed his hearing. Perhaps he would hear himself better in the dark.

Yet nothing came. How little he knew of Ben, where he lived, under what roof he slept, what family—if any— he had in London.

He noticed then a small group clustered by Blackfriars Bridge. All warmed their hands over smudge pots as they listened to an apothecary read aloud by torchlight. Charles drew closer. To his great gratification, this charmed circle heeded a reading of <u>A Christmas Carol</u>. Abashed, Dickens stepped back into the shadows and watched.

He did not recognize one of the listeners—Paige Knight. Paige, who had followed Dickens the past hour, feigned deep interest in the reading. Only when it ended did one of the audience look up and see Charley in the background. "On the stone of Scone!" he exclaimed. "I'd swear it's Father Christmas!"

All heads turned in Charley's direction. The ecstatic group then arose and swarmed as one the ambushed author. They surged about him, slapping him on the back, wishing him well and "Merry Christmas!" He denied many times his identity, but they knew him well, knew his likeness from the papers and from seeing Twist's author stalking their streets.

Buoyed by the joy he inspired in these people,

Charley exploited the situation as he must. Did any of them know Ben Newborn? Had anybody seen the lad lately? One little urchin identified Paige as a friend of Ben's. Hearing this, Paige stepped back into shadows.

So Dickens approached Paige. They sized each other up. Neither seemed please by the sight of the other, but Charles ignored their mutual distaste. "I must find Ben," he said in low voice. "Please, do you know where he is?"

Paige studied this man whom she had never before met. She did not like what she saw. Dickens wore fancy clothes and was much too clean. Besides, he had charges to press against Benjamin, for stealing the gold leaf. She wondered if Dickens knew about that yet. Did he know he was talking to Ben's accomplice?

"Dunno where he is." That was all Paige said. It was the truth, although no one would ever believe it. Dickens glared at the girl. She stubbornly kept her stand. "You're wasting your time, sir. Newborn's been nabbed by the law."

"No he hasn't!" Dickens nearly bowled Paige over with the ferocity of his tone.

"How do you know that, sir? You can't know that!" She tried but failed to hide her relief at hearing this news.

"I certainly do! I've spent my day at the courts and at Newgate. They don't have Benjamin—at least not yet. And I need to find him before the law does. Oh, why didn't he come to me straightaway? If only he hadn't left the invoice and run!"

Taken aback, Paige asked, "You spent the day looking for Benjamin? At the prison and the likes?" Her voice cracked.

"Yes!" Dickens fumed. "I know everybody in the prison system, so take my word for it. Now, will you help me!"

Paige mulled this development just as a swirl of people suddenly picked up and grew like a breeze turned stiff wind off the river. Voices called, beckoned to one another. Over and over, the man and girl heard: "It's for the queen! It's for the queen!" Curiosity overcoming them, Paige and Dickens let themselves be swept up and carried away toward the road by the river.

Clop, clop, jingle, jangle. The plodding of shod hooves grew sharper, closer. Louder, too, grew the rattling of equestrian fittings — stirrup irons, martingales, saber scabbards, bells. Horses nickering, snorting, sneezing . . . the grinding of wagon wheels on a rubble-strewn street . . . the groaning of a wagon laden to its limit.

In an instant, a contingent of cavalry burst into view, the officers resplendent in their scarlet jackets, their matching saddle blankets embossed in gold.

Awed, Paige asked, "What's those soldiers?"

"Royal Horse Guards," Dickens answered. "You can tell by the uniforms. They serve Her Majesty, the queen."

"Oh!" said a bedazzled Paige Knight.

What followed beguiled the crowd even more: a half dozen Shire horses pulling an enormous dray. The size and beauty of these splendid animals drew exclamations from the crowd. Shires were the largest horses in all the world. Their feathered feet, the size of soup plates, set small piles of snow into flight.

Paige whistled. Then Dickens grabbed her by the shoulder. "See what's on the dray!" he shouted.

The elite cavalry and magic horses transported a twenty-foot-tall Scottish pine.

The crowd cheered its approval—as did Dickens. Paige couldn't understand the event transpiring, and with Dickens shouting, it was all hard to fathom. Impatient, she demanded: "Why they hauling a dead tree around? Is everybody buggy?"

"Don't you know!" said Dickens, cheering. "It's a Christmas tree! The prince Albert must have asked for it. They love Christmas in his home country, and I promise you he's asked for this first of royal *Tannenbaums!* Isn't it wonderful! The queen's bringing Christmas back to the palace!"

Jubilant as a child, Dickens forgot for a moment his plight.

Paige looked about her. She almost didn't recognize these poor people she knew, carrying on like enraptured children who'd never known a woe. They all owed this moment of unbridled happiness to the madcap author in the clashing vest and jacket. They owed it to this Charles

Dickens, who had searched all afternoon through gaol cells for Ben — not to hurt him but to give him a hand.

Paige's head hurt.

She tugged at Dickens's elbow. Charles turned round.

"Sir, Ben couldn't go to you himself. He couldn't face you."

"But why? We could have solved the entire matter together!"

Paige sighed. "I need to tell you about the two of us."

Dickens gave her his full attention. "What about you two?"

Paige felt sick as she explained, "We was stealing from you. Gold leaf. I fenced it for Ben. That's why he couldn't go to you and come clean. We're guilty as Dick Turpin of highway robbery. I've got no idea where he is now, none at all. And that's the truth."

Charley's face fell. He said very quietly, "Ben was stealing from me too, eh?"

"Honest, he didn't know you was paying for the gold stuff until after we'd started." Paige hated herself for having to say this.

Dickens looked at her askance. "When you found out I was paying for it, what happened then?"

Paige shrugged. "Ben wanted to stop. Not me. I wouldn't agree, so he ran. This is my doin'. You can lock me up, sir. I done Newgate once. I can handle it. Not

Ben. Do what you can for him. He's got the whole world to look forward to."

Dismay cleft Charley's heart in two. He looked at Paige, so deeply attached to Ben, so incapable of hiding the depth of her feelings. He also realized that Paige hadn't grasped her friend's predicament. Whether or not Dickens should disclose to Paige the whole truth tugged him in opposite directions. While he didn't wish to scare her needlessly, playing games with Paige could insure disaster.

"Come, child. Sit with me. Just for a moment." Dickens spoke to her in the same gentle manner he used in speaking to his own daughter Mamie.

Paige's distrust reasserted herself. She pulled away. Dickens pushed, "Your Ben might not have any world to look forward to if you and I don't act as partners. *Now.*" That did it. Paige hoisted herself onto a low stone wall and listened intently to Dickens, who sat down beside her.

With enormous difficulty, he explained to Paige that the charges against Ben carried frightful weight in court. It was one thing for street urchins to steal the necessities of life. It was another matter entirely for them to stand accused of theft, embezzlement, and forgery by two well-established men of trade. If Squib and Ledrook found Ben and testified against him, Ben would be hung in due haste. The publishers probably wouldn't tell Dickens so that he might speak on Ben's behalf. The magistrate would close the case within minutes.

Paige had lost her mother, her father, her brother. She tried to comprehend that she might also lose Ben, that he would not merely be consigned to a cell at Newgate but taken to the press-yard and killed. So terrible was this shock that she could not even cry. Numbly Paige offered, "He said he was going to see some man who'd have to turn him in. He didn't say who. He wouldn't tell. That's all I know, sir. I swear that's all."

With a vacant look, she stared into space. With all his might, Dickens tried to fathom Ben's words to Paige, but he couldn't make sense of any of them. If Ben had surrendered himself, Dickens would have found him—in Newgate, Old Bailey, the courts.

As Dickens silently labored over this riddle, tears started trickling from Paige's pain-stricken eyes. He heard her sniffle. Without even looking over, he reached out and clasped in his gloved right hand her callused, grimy left paw. She broke down, sobs wracking her body.

No one had ever before held her hand.

CHAPTER TWELVE

While Charles searched London, One Devonshire transformed into a home for Father Christmas. The short little fir from the garden decorated the drawing room, its limbs laden with Mamie's and young Charley's handicrafts. Ivy garlands bedecked the first floor while sprigs of holly and mistletoe added grace notes of color. A Yule log burned in the hearth, its flames crackling and snapping against the cold.

Upstairs, Catherine labeled a parcel she had just tied with string. Its addressee: Mr. Washington Irving. In the kitchen, Mrs. Plimpton sampled sauces aboil on the stove in the cinnamon-scented kitchen.

Boodle helped, too. He tidied Charley's study, clearing the side tables, throwing out old journals. He espied on the desk a sloppy pile of bills. Squinting, he could not read at the top of each the words "Ledrook and Squib." Shrugging, Boodle slid the entire accounting pile into a wastebasket, which he then took outside and emptied in a trash bin.

When Charles came home that evening, he opened the door to his own private wonderland. The children vied for his attention in bragging about marvels they had made for Christmas; but one person stole the show. Catherine, radiant and recovered from the previous month's rigors, stepped gingerly down the staircase. Wearing a green velvet dress and a sash of the Hogarth tartan, she looked the very picture of Mrs. Christmas.

Charles, Mrs. Plimpton, little Charley, and Mamie burst into a chorus of applause and "Brava!" They made a triumphal procession into the dining room, where a Noel feast awaited them. Roast beef, Stilton cheese, plum puddings topped with holly—these dishes and more sat on the sideboard. Even little Walter, seated in his high chair, joined the party. Once all had gathered round at the table, Catherine rang her Spode bell. Boodle, on cue, entered bearing on a platter a twelve-pound turkey.

"Mrs. Dickens, wherever did you find that bird!" said Charles, decidedly taken by surprise. Catherine revealed that the tom came courtesy of another Tom—Carlyle. It was a Christmas gift to the real "Cratchit family."

With trembling hands, Boodle picked up a carving knife and aimed himself at the turkey. Dickens dashed to his side. "That's quite all right, Boodle! I'll do the honors." The butler sighed in deep relief and returned, with Mrs. Plimpton, to the kitchen.

The little Dickenses all talked or gurgled as befitted their age while Mrs. Dickens cooed at each. Dickens made short shrift of the turkey, carving it with precision. Then he stopped. On impulse he picked up one, then another, side chair and placed these at the table. He grabbed from the sideboard two place settings of silver, dishes, and goblets. These he set on the table, then disappeared into the kitchen.

Confused, little Charley looked after his father. "Mummy, what is Daddy doing?"

Catherine didn't even look up. "Darling, I've learned not to ask."

Dickens returned with Boodle and Minnie Plimpton in tow. He escorted his housekeeper to one empty place and seated her. Then he led his bewildered butler to a setting at the right hand of Mrs. Dickens. "Sit!" Dickens commanded.

Boodle, looking lost, didn't respond. "Go on, sit, sit, sit!" Dickens commanded. Boodle sat. With unblinking eyes, he glanced at his master and sighed, for once, from bliss. No one had ever seen Boodle wear such a look of contentment. He seemed a different person.

Catherine, glowing from an inner light, raised her water glass in a toast to her husband. "We have so much to celebrate. In just one week, all six thousand copies of <u>A Christmas Carol</u> have sold." All but Charles clapped or squealed. Catherine continued, "We who sit at his table and share his life are indeed blessed. Bravo, Charles! Your star has again risen and now shines on the lowly this holy night."

All raised their water goblets, Mrs. Plimpton boosting Walter's bottle. Smiling weakly, Dickens then accepted his homage — and sat down to the worst holiday dinner of his life.

Everyone was so cheerful and happy as Dickens struggled to hide his true mood. He grinned and nodded and picked at his plate. Within he heard a riot of clashing voices: Squib taunting him with "What profits?" Or Carlyle warning, "It could be a hoax . . . You must have a witness! You must!" Or Cromwell thundering, "Poverty is your birthright. Your inescapable fate!" The voices grew louder, dissolving into a chorus of doubt and scorn, fear and doom.

Catherine studied her husband without being obvious about it. Yes, Charley looked odd. He was talking to himself, she knew. Then fell the coup de grâce. He had heard in his head the scornful John Dickens say, "Enjoying the life of a liar? Ha! You're a poor man's son and you'll be poor again—like me."

"That does it!" Dickens shouted, and shot to his feet. Silence descended upon the table. "I'm going for a walk. I'll be back when I'm back!" With that, Charley stormed from the room. Catherine, oblivious to her husband's outburst, picked up a serving dish and passed it to her right. "Mr. Boodle, would you care for some stuffing?"

Dickens rushed down a street of chic brick homes. In his wake trailed Thomas, arguing volubly and with virtually each step. "This is fine thanks for the turkey I sent you, dragging me through Kensington at this hour of the night." Thomas had been happily ensconced in his garden, puffing on the pipe his wife had forbidden him to smoke indoors. No sooner had he settled down for some postprandial contemplations than Charles had stormed through the door of 24 Cheyne Row. He had implored Thomas to accompany him on a mission of utmost importance.

Torn between comfort and curiosity, Thomas had finally opted to support his friend on this crazed crusade to Kensingon.

They walked right up to the front door of one row house, where Charley banged hard on the door with his fist. While Carlyle stewed, the door swung open to show Josiah Squib standing in his foyer. "Well, well, Merry Christmas to you, Charles!"

Dickens, without a word, strode inside, followed by Thomas. Feeling awkward, Carlyle muttered, "To you, too, Josiah."

The Squib home exuded the air of a residence decorated with the remainders of estate sales. Georgian, Regency, and early Victorian horrors cluttered the hallways and rooms. Through one open door Charley glimpsed the Squib and Ledrook families dining and chatting gaily. Josiah cautioned his visitor, "Now, Charles, remember: Peace on earth, good will toward men, and don't throw a tantrum at a formal dinner party."

Ignoring him, Charles pointed at Rufus. "I want to see Josiah and you in private — now!"

Rufus called out, "You'd ruin our pineapple creams."

Charley hissed at Josiah, "Fine, we'll join you instead. I'd prefer that your families hear what I have to say."

Josiah gave him a toothy, utterly mendacious grin. "Of course, Charles. In my study!"

In Squib's study, crammed with books and papers, the two sides squared off for a duel: Josiah to one side, Charley to the other, Rufus and Thomas their respective seconds. Squib insisted one more time, "Charles, you've gone round the bend. There is no such invoice. Never was."

Rufus chimed in, "One hundred sixty-eight pounds for advertising is a sum so preposterous, not a single soul will believe you."

Squib smelled a rat. "I don't understand, Charles. We have yet to give you an invoice for advertising."

"What if I'd seen it with my own eyes?" Charles replied.

"Then I'd say you needed spectacles. How did you see it?" asked Josiah.

Rufus retorted, "Any such invoice was obviously, ah, a fake!"

Josiah slapped his forehead. "Of course it was! That thieving little guttersnipe! You must have seen that false set of papers we found in the printers' shack. Oh, dear me. We learned the hard way how literate that rascal really is. Why, he's a master forger! That's why we've had to warn the public. Heavens, he could fool the Bank of England."

Rufus rued, "Beastly business, isn't it?"

As he spoke, Dickens focused on the pattern of the Oriental carpet underfoot. "You're both lying, gentlemen. Benjamin did not forge that invoice. Why on earth would he have done such a thing? You did it, Josiah. I know your hand as well as you know mine. Besides, I haven't just seen the phony invoice. I have it. Pay me every pound and penny of profits owed or I sue your firm and we meet in a court of law. Until then, do not even think of seizing my plates as compensation for debts. Understood? By the way, I've been to Pimlico Paperworks. I've had a talk with their bookkeeper."

Josiah and Rufus tried not to look at each other but failed. Dickens caught their glance. Josiah made a bid for time. "Certainly there might be some discrepancies, but we can clear those up at the appropriate time. All you've done so far is wreck our holiday dinner and slander both Rufus and me. This is intolerable! Look at all we have done for you, and in return, you would defame us. Careful or we shall be the parties to institute legal action!"

Rufus jumped right in. "Don't forget. You used our vendors and employees. We have a reputation to maintain. Had you defaulted on payments to our suppliers and workers, you would have discredited us. We risked our professional necks for you!"

Josiah closed in for the kill. "Quite a risk, too. You're known to be penny-wise and pound-foolish. Look at your fancy dwellings. No, you'll someday end up at the Marshalsea just like your ignoble father."

Dickens stepped back as though struck. Carlyle bellowed, "Don't stand for that, Charles! That was slander and I heard it myself. How dare you utter such infamy!" fumed Carlyle.

Looking martyred, Josiah asked, "Well, Charles. Am I lying?"

For the moment, Dickens swallowed his mortification. "On that point, no, sir."

Carlyle, who knew nothing of Dickens's father, gave his friend a double take. Over insults less than this, duels were fought. Carlyle, however, misread Charley's priorities.

In a magnanimous-sounding offer of peace, Josiah—palms up and raised heavenward—offered, "Rufus and I are willing to forgive these scurrilous attacks on our good names if you agree, Charles, to drop this whole matter. Not another word about any of it!"

Having concealed his ulterior goal, Charles let drop as casually as he could, "Why don't we just have Newborn in here and ask him about the whole business. Let's clear the air. I'm willing."

Neither side knew where Benjamin was, and neither wished to give that fact away. Ben was useful to each—for very different reasons. This stalemate brought the confrontation to a dead halt, a wall clock ticking too loudly, Ledrook's stomach grumbling quite audibly. Out of this impasse, no exit emerged.

"This is a case for the Bow Street Runners!" muttered Carlyle to Dickens. He referred to a corps of private detectives founded in 1750 and supplanted by the City of London's police. However, he might as well had said to Dickens, "Abracadabra!" or "Open Sesame!" so amazed did Charley look.

Charley asked too quietly of Josiah, "You reported your charges to the London police?"

"Well, of course we went to the authorities!" replied Squib.

Dickens didn't know whether to believe him, but it didn't matter. He tugged at Carlyle's elbow. "Gentlemen, if you will excuse us, I should really consult with a solicitor before discussing these matters any further. Cheerio!"

Carlyle, beyond befuddlement, uttered, "Ta!" and hastened with Dickens from the study. Behind them, Squib called, "You'll be hearing from our solicitor, too, I tell you!"

"What's gotten into those two? They're behaving rather oddly," said Rufus, tugging at the loose skin of his chin.

Josiah gave Rufus a baleful look. "I think we have just lost the most beloved author in England."

"I thought you were trying to lose his business!"

Josiah slumped into his chair. "Benjamin was limp, but it's your brain that's lame. Where is that blasted boy anyway? He can't hide from us forever. Oh, why did I let you talk me into this?"

"Me?" said Rufus, genuinely offended. "Just who forged the invoices, you scavenging bird of prey? I should file charges — against you!"

Josiah sneered, "You pompous, prevaricating wind-bag!"

Rufus glowered. "You even look like a vulture. In a graveyard is where you'll find dessert."

Josiah waved his hand at the garden door. "Oh, go on, go on. Make yourself at home in the garden. I've needed someone to root out the truffles. Then again, you'd hog the trough . . . "

The two continued throughout the night to find ever lower levels on which to express their newfound and mutual contempt.

Fatigued from tearing about London on foot, Carlyle insisted that they hire a cab to their next destination. As their two-wheeled hansom thumped its way riverward, Dickens clarified one point. He, Squib, Ledrook—all had made the same mistake. The London police had jurisdiction only over the City itself. Whitechapel, however, lay outside that jurisdiction; so did the publishing firm, though only by a block or two.

Further, Paige reported that Ben intended to turn himself in to some authority. They had simply erred on his point of surrender.

At a canter, the cabbie's horse careened right through the royal borough of Westminster to the front door of 4 Whitehall Place. This night the elephantine structure hinted of its fabled past. Icicles hung like stalactites from the eaves. Snow frosted the windows and mansard roof, the normally gray building cloaked in pristine white. Glittering under starlight and the face of a full moon, Whitehall looked like an ice palace from the pole.

"What's this? Where are we?" Carlyle asked.

The cabbie paid, Dickens replied, "Scotland Yard."

Like most cultivated Londoners, Carlyle had no idea what Peel's metropolitan force actually did. Its jurisdiction lay outside the limits of the City of London itself. Many believed these bobbies were just agents for controlling the rabble—spies, snitches, stoolies, another social experiment of Sir Robert's.

Dickens knew not what to expect. He and Carlyle might as well have called on the Exchequer. The constables did not wear uniforms, save for their high stiff hats on which they could stand and peek over walls. With few on duty this Christmas Eve, the building seemed eerily empty, footsteps ricocheting down corridors. At the end of one hall, a sergeant sat perched at a high desk. His mustache, bushy brows, and balding head gave him the appearance of a well-fed walrus.

Dickens approached and introduced himself. The sergeant glowered. "We've been expecting you. Follow me!"

Filled with foreboding, Charley and Thomas followed the bobbie round the corner and into the office of Inspector Spright. He, too, wore everyday clothes and looked to Dickens more like an elf than a man. The inspector stood, which was hard to tell as he barely cleared five feet in height. The officer shook hands with the visitors. "You're here about Newborn, I take it?"

"Yes!" Dickens exclaimed. "I must speak on his behalf!"

"Coffee? A tot of rum?" the little fellow asked cheerfully.

Before Dickens could decline, Carlyle interjected, "A tot for me, thank you." The inspector directed his sergeant to fetch them the potables, then instructed his callers to sit. Quite calmly he announced, "We've taken care of Newborn."

"What have you done with him?" Dickens demanded.

"Can't say just yet. You'll need to fill out a report."

"A report?" Dickens pleaded, "Is he *safe*?"

Swinging in a heartbeat from merry to canny, Inspector Spright picked up a sheet of foolscap and read from it aloud: "I have the satisfaction of knowing that there is not a single law connected with my name which has not had as its object some mitigation of the criminal law, some prevention of abuse in the exercise of it." He put down the paper and asked, "Do you know who wrote that?"

"Hammurabi?" Carlyle guessed.

"Wrong!" beamed the bobbie. "That was our

founder, Sir Robert Peel." He let that sink in before explaining, "Your Newborn stands accused of theft, yet we can't understand what it is that he actually stole. Mr. Dickens, is the book <u>A Christmas Carol</u> your property?"

"It certainly is!"

"It is not, then, the property of Ledrook and Squib?"

Dickens caught the inspector's direction. "Correct! They can't claim he stole a book from them. It wasn't their book in the first place."

"Hmmm. Neither do we know or have evidence of anything Newborn forged or embezzled. Mr. Dickens, do you support the allegations made by the publishing firm of Ledrook and Squib?"

"They're poppycock and I can prove it!" Charley averred.

"Hmm. I'll make a note of that. He also says that he stole from you. True?"

Charley's heart sank. He thought carefully before responding with, "I have no direct evidence of any such theft."

"Hmm. So you have no charges to press?"

Dickens shook his head firmly. "I do not."

"Well then, what's the fuss? Mr. Dickens, coffee?" The sergeant had arrived with a full-service tray. Dickens still wasn't told Ben's whereabouts, but he agreed to fill out a long report for the bobbies. This took half an hour. Carlyle, happy with his grog, then witnessed Charley's statement on the entire affair. Inspector

Spright suggested quite helpfully that Ledrook and Squib desist from taking Ben's good name in vain . . . or else.

That was how Charles Dickens and Thomas Carlyle came to spend Christmas Eve at Scotland Yard and how the people of London first learned that their bobbies were sometimes angels.

A cab deposited Dickens and Carlyle at the foot of One Devonshire. Carlyle decided that after this wild night of goose chasing, he should pay his respects in person to Catherine. Dickens, loitering at the curb, seemed reluctant to enter the house. Carlyle didn't even want to know what bothered him. He told his friend, "If there's more on your mind, save it. I've had enough for one night."

With that, Thomas grabbed the handrail and stepped up. He paused, however, when he saw charging up Marylebone Road an awfully familiar team of horses pulling a carriage fit for a prince. He whispered to Charles, "Look at that!" Dickens whipped around and saw a magnificent closed carriage pulled by white Hackneys four-in-hand. "Oh . . . my . . . word!" chanted Carlyle.

The transport stopped at Charley's home. A footman alit and opened the carriage door. From it descended a nearly unrecognizable person. Handsomely groomed and finely attired, Benjamin James Newborn stepped out. On the ground he turned round to thank the carriage occupants. In the lamplight Charles and Thomas saw that the vehicle transported Sir Robert and Lady Julia Peel.

Carlyle fell back and struck his head against a lamp-post.

"Merry Christmas, Master Newborn!" Lady Julia called.

"Merry Christmas, m'lady. And to you, Sir Robert."

Sir Robert gave Dickens an enigmatic smile, then ordered his driver to "Carry on!" The horses clamped their bits and sprung forward, floating like ghosts into the night.

Dickens realized — Ben had surrendered to Sir Robert himself. How he had managed that, Charley wanted to know.

So many emotions then descended upon Dickens that he was unable to vocalize. Fatigue, relief, awe, joy, all battered at once his overused brain. He watched as Ben, without a crutch, walked up the stairs and to the door. In his hands he held a copy of Charley's book. He handed this to Dickens. "This belongs to you, sir. There's something else you need to know."

Feeling deliciously smug, Dickens let slip, "Oh, I know all about your sticky fingers and the gold leaf. Paige told me."

"Paige!" The table of surprise had turned swiftly on Benjamin. "How did she get into this!"

Dickens savored the moment. "Come in, lad. All you

owe me—" He paused to think "—is the unedited, unabridged story."

Ben hesitated before arguing, "Sir, I must see Alice. And Paige. They need me . . . "

"Hush!" ordered Charles. "Paige is with Alice. They're safe. Spend Christmas Day with them. Christmas Eve, you owe *me*."

So Benjamin followed Dickens and Carlyle into the house. In the drawing room, festivities awaited them. Dozens of well-wishers had dropped by throughout the night. An accordionist and a fiddler played polkas for the children while the giant John Leech taught tiny Mamie to dance. In the riotous atmosphere, Charles drew Catherine aside and regaled her with the evening's adventures.

Little Charley interrupted his parents when he begged of his father a magic act. He happily obliged.

With the approach of midnight, Carlyle stood to one side and observed. He thought back to that fortuitous day on which Charley Dickens had addressed the House of Commons. That was the same day on which they had met Benjamin Newborn—the prime minister's new foundling. Now everybody knew the facts: Newborn had saved Dickens by placing in Sir Robert's hands a copy of the book. His brave, daring, reckless deed had started all the commotion.

With this comforting notion swaddling his soul, Carlyle looked about the room, savoring the sights. He wondered if he could carry, for the balance of his days, his sense that into this room came a powerful light, passing from father to son, from Charles to Ben, and through ink and pen to hearths across the kingdom—wherever a child's light was welcome, at home.

Scarcely three weeks passed before Catherine delivered safely into the world a healthy baby boy. Charles had decided on Christmas Eve to name this child for his sister, Frances, and so the infant was christened Francis Jeffrey. It no longer mattered to Dickens that, as a homeless child, he had toiled in a blacking factory while Frances advanced at the Royal Music Academy.

That was all a long, long time ago.

. . . And Christmas had come, at last, to One Devonshire.

a c k n o w l e d g m e n t s

Since the night my mother first suggested this tale, I have associated with several persons whose story consulting, ideas, critiques, and stylistic tips have significantly improved the project: Henry Bloomstein, Jack Allen, Ken Atchity, Robert Barnett, Benjamin Caswell, Capt. Hugh Cleave RN, Daniel Dumas, Monica Faulkner, Tom John, Richard Lederer, Rick Rosen, Tim Scott, Everett M. Sims, Michael Standing, Helen Sues, and Stanford Whitmore. I also thank Paxton Whitehead, actor and friend, whose Britannic majesty of a voice resounds in the dialogue of several characters. Others provided indispensable counsel and comfort: Cathy Ann Bencivengo, Jeanine and Brian Bennett, Mary Boehm, Scott and Sabrina Davis, Kirk Frederick, Michael Laughlin, Louis C. Mone, Samuel Newborn, Father

Jerry O'Donnell, Alison Tibbitts, Cindy Tillinghast, Nancy Young, Karl ZoBell, and the staff of AEI.

Seraphim wings are reserved for my unfailingly generous and gracious editor, Jennifer Weis of St. Martin's Press, without whom this book would not exist. In like fashion, I am indebted to the supremely gifted Chi-Li Wong whose splendid suggestions for this story and exacting, chapter-by-chapter analysis of the manuscript brought me to a new level of writing skill. I would also salute the legions of foot soldiers in the ever-widening war on illiteracy, particularly Chris McFadden, a personal hero and modern-day miracle worker as chief of the San Diego Public Library's adult literacy program.

During these years, I lost my Wise Men, mentors who graced my days with Magus-like insight and bountiful faith: Paul R. Picard; William B. Perkins, S.J.; Father I. Brent Eagen. They loved this story. I'd like to think of it as a stained-glass window through which their light might shine.

a b o u t   t h e   a u t h o r

PATRICIA K. DAVIS is a resident of San Diego County.
A Midnight Carol is her first novel.